PUTHAM HOUSE

Hephzibah Jesudasan is a native of Pulipunam, Kanyakumari district, Tamil Nadu. She spent her early years in Burma, where her father worked. After the outbreak of the Second World War, her family had to leave Burma and rebuild their life in Pulipunam, which became the wellspring of her creative energy. A gentle and unassuming figure, Hephzibah Jesudasan straddled the world of Tamil and English Literature with ease. After completing her BA (Honours) in English from Maharaja's University College, Trivandrum, she went on to work as a professor of English. An accomplished translator, essayist, novelist, poet and writer of children's books, she took to writing in Tamil encouraged by her husband Jesudasan, who was a renowned professor of Tamil himself. Her works are memorable for her artless prose and earnest portrayal of the palmyra climbers of her region. Her first novel *Putham Veedu* (1964) is celebrated as an important forerunner of the realistic novel in Tamil. *Ma Ni, Anathai* and *Dr Chellappan* are three of her other novels. Her book *The Tamils Down the Ages through their Literature* is considered to have made significant contributions in tracing the history of Tamil writing.

G. Geetha has a master's degree in English from Loyola College, Madras University. After teaching English for ten years, she is now a freelance translator based in Chennai.

PUTHAM HOUSE

Hephzibah Jesudasan
Translated by **G. Geetha**

Published by
Rupa Publications India Pvt. Ltd 2021
7/16, Ansari Road, Daryaganj
New Delhi 110002

Sales Centres:

Allahabad Bengaluru Chennai
Hyderabad Jaipur Kathmandu
Kolkata Mumbai

Copyright © J. Thambi Thangakumaran 2021
Translation copyright © G. Geetha 2021

Published by arrangement with Kalachuvadu Publications.

This is a work of fiction. Names, characters, places and incidents are either the product of the author's imagination or are used fictitiously and any resemblance to any actual person, living or dead, events or locales is entirely coincidental.
The contents of this book reflect the views of the author and translator. The Tamilnadu Textbook and Educational Services Corporation is not responsible for the same.

All rights reserved.
No part of this publication may be reproduced, transmitted, or stored in a retrieval system, in any form or by any means, electronic, mechanical, photocopying, recording or otherwise, without the prior permission of the publisher.

ISBN: 978-93-5520-025-9

First impression 2021

10 9 8 7 6 5 4 3 2 1

Printed at Repro India Limited, Haryana

This book is sold subject to the condition that it shall not, by way of trade or otherwise, be lent, resold, hired out, or otherwise circulated, without the publisher's prior consent, in any form of binding or cover other than that in which it is published.

MISSION STATEMENT

This is an initiative of the Tamil Nadu Textbook and Educational Services Corporation (TNTB & ESC) under the aegis of GO. Ms. No. 207, SE(TRB) Dept., Dated 22.09.2017, action plan 6, to identify and translate into English, Tamil literary works, that they might enhance the reach of Tamil antiquity, tradition and contemporaneity and enrich world literature to also translate significant literary voices for other languages into Tamil. Both ventures are to be undertaken as either an independent or joint publications with collaborating publishers.

Members, Academic Advising Committee (Translation)
1. Dr R. Balakrishnan, IAS, Researcher and Writer
2. Thiru. S. Ramakrishnan, Writer
3. Thiru. S. Madasamy, Educationist

Project Execution Team
1. Thiru. Dindigul I. Leoni, Chairperson, TNTB & ESC
2. Dr D. Manikandan IAS, Managing Director, TNTB & ESC
3. Dr S. Kannappan, Member Secretary, TNTB & ESC
4. Thiru. R. Dhayalan, Financial Advisor, TNTB & ESC
5. Dr T.S. Saravanan, Deputy Director (Translation), TNTB & ESC
6. Thiru. K. Subramani, Deputy Director (Publications), TNTB & ESC
7. Thiru. M. Appanasamy, Consultant, TNTB & ESC
8. Tmt. Mini Krishnan, Co-ordinating Editor, TNTB & ESC

Contents

1. Putham House — 1
2. Two Brothers — 7
3. The Sparrow — 15
4. The Mission House — 23
5. Imprisonment — 28
6. The Palmyra Climbing Season — 38
7. A Measure of Rope — 49
8. The Relations from Town — 63
9. Lizzy-Lily — 83
10. The Illness and the Cure — 105
11. Crime and Punishment — 127
12. The Verdict — 150

Remembering My Mother — 168
Glossary — 173

1
Putham House

In Panaivilai there is nothing but palmyra trees, thickets and thickets of them stretching as far as the eye can see. Every now and then, you hear the rustle of the fronds. And through that, another sound—as if someone is playing with the hardy palm stalks, striking one with another. These toddy palms—*appappa*! How they look! At times even frightening! How did this tree get to be so tall? The palmyra, you could say, is the Goliath among trees. Such is its height. When the wind blows hard, its head, crowned with a wreath of bright green leaves, seems to be in a whirl. But you should look at its trunk—all craggy and blackened. It is nothing but stone, hard stone, tough and unyielding. You can't clasp it even if you wrapped both your arms around it. From a distance, though, the palmyras look like slender threads, pitch black, swaying playfully, white clouds nestling on their crowns. Such an illusion! The fronds atop the tree flutter like crow's wings.

The ground here is a carpet of green. A tangle of weeds and grass, nothing else. Thorny bushes thrive in plenty. And wherever your feet tread, the shy and shrinking *thotta chinungi*—the touch-me-nots. There is a profusion of another wild shrub too—*puchedi*, they call it. All flowering plants are puchedi, so it is strange this shrub should be specially called by this name. It is covered with teeny-weeny red flowers glittering like ear studs made of rubies. It appears that no one gathers these flowers to adorn their hair with. All the same, they are such wonderful playthings for the children. Amid all this dense undergrowth—bush, bramble and blossom—there is hardly any trace of cultivation. Not a single pulse or grain, not even leafy greens. It is evident that these village folk care very little about farming.

Nevertheless, there is no dearth of abundance. Lush mango trees stand here and there. One look at the laden trees during the fruit-bearing season is enough to say that they are of the wild sort. The crows circling a couple of jackfruit trees are making such a ruckus. On closer inspection, it appears that they are cawing out an invitation for a jackfruit feast. Besides the scent of mushy jackfruit pods scattered on the ground, the air is suffused with another pleasant fragrance. All you have to do is close your eyes and inhale deeply. It is the sweet smell of *punnai* flowers, there's no mistaking it.

There are signs of nature's bounty everywhere. Perhaps this is why the village folk hardly think of shedding their sweat in toil. As for the birds, they have such a merry time. *Adey Appa!* So many kinds of birds and what a medley of noises they make! How they warble, twitter, chirp and cry raucously! And through all this, the shrill screech of squirrels. There goes a squirrel, chasing another up a palm tree. A chameleon that had been lying all the while in the shade stretches its neck gingerly into the sunlight. Oh, the sight of it changing colours! Beautiful beyond words!

Then there is another creature—slippery like a snake and swift as an arrow. It has three stripes on its back, just like the squirrel. Everyone flinches in fear at the mere sight of it. This is the one they call the *aranai*. There is even a popular saying around these parts, 'Scour half the kingdom, search as you might, there's no cure for the aranai's bite'. But were you to inquire if anyone has ever died of its bite, the answer is an emphatic 'no'. Be that as it may, it is a poisonous creature according to popular lore. It is such a common sight, yet you must step aside instantly if you see one. On the other hand, it is said that there are several really harmful snakes here. Not to mention the countless folk tales about them. It seems the young ones of the *anali*—the deadly viper—hatch from their mother's stomach, ripping it apart in the process. The *sarai*—the rat snake—is believed to be the consort of the cobra. But since snakes love the dark, one hardly gets to see them in the day. Nevertheless, their shadow, not unlike a vague fear, flits across one's heart all the time.

In fact, there are many such nameless fears. Ghosts and spirits play a considerable part in rustic life. The spirit of a man who died falling from a palm haunts the tree, or so they say. In the month of *Karthigai*, ghosts set out holding aloft a flaming torch. Pregnant women must never venture out after dark lest a ghost cast its shadow on them. In some places, betel nuts grow all of a sudden on the *ithil* vines. You have only to strike the spot with an axe and you are sure to find gold. Speaking of which, it seems ghosts are frightened of iron axes, so you must never forget to carry one.

This is the setting. In the midst of all this stands a large, ancient house. But the villagers call it Putham Veedu, the 'new house.' It is huge and rambling, in near ruins, falling apart like the lives of its inhabitants. It has a tiled roof. Now, finding a house with a tiled roof in such a small village isn't all that easy, is it? The black, moss-covered tiles trumpet its past grandeur, while the walls are in a pitiful state. Who knows how many years have passed since they were last whitewashed? They are cracked, the mud plaster crumbling here and there.

In front of the house runs an *adichukootu*—a long verandah. Built as a retreat in the hot summer months, it is not tiled but simply thatched over with dried palm leaves. One look at the weather-beaten palm leaves is enough to confirm that the roof was not meant for the rainy season. The wooden pillars along the adichukootu are dilapidated and worn out, threatening to fall at any moment. But you must look at the main door that leads into the house from the adichukootu. It is an ornamental door made of fine teakwood, tough as steel. Even after so many years, and in spite of the black layers of dust covering it, the fine decorative carvings stand out, a proof of the workmanship of the artisan who made it. Masons, they say, build a house only after carefully considering all the aspects that ensure the flow of wealth and prosperity. Perhaps the mason who built this house made an error in his calculations. Who knows?

The ageing patriarch of the house is fast asleep on a makeshift cot made of two benches, his head resting on a large, soiled pillow. Outside, the sun is blazing hot. But that hardly seems to affect the old man. The sound of his snoring is quite loud. Flies hover over his face, disturbing his otherwise deep sleep. He involuntarily flutters the palm *visiri* in his right hand from time to time. And every now and then his snoring stops.

The old man, asleep on the cot, looks very much like a lean palm tree himself. His hands and legs are sturdy and well built. He shows no signs of frailty even at this age. His head is smooth, shaped like an egg, and his unkempt beard is peppered with white hair. A dirty dhoti is all he is wearing. His feet stick six inches out of the cot and hang suspended in the air.

In a little while, he stirs awake and calls out in his heavy, hoarse voice, 'Ei!' As there is no response from the house but for the noise of the wooden pestle, he bellows louder, 'Ei, can't you hear?' In reply, a small girl comes running. She makes a little place for herself on the narrow bench and nestles close to the old man.

'What is it, *Kannapachi*?'

The moment he sees the little girl, the old man's eyes soften with affection.

'Is it you, my dear? Fetch a glass of buttermilk from that old woman. Can't hear these days, the old hag. Go, child!'

The girl hesitates for a while. 'Kannapachi, *Kannammai* is busy. That's why she didn't hear you calling.'

The old man smiles gently and kisses her forehead. 'How well you defend her! Did you learn this at school as well?' he asks, proud of her. At once she jumps up and skips into the house.

2

Two Brothers

The little girl is Lizzy. Picture a child of ten with a cheerful face, sparkling eyes, dusky complexion and a bounce in her steps. Her mother kept repeating, 'Kutty, you are a girl. Is this any way for a girl to behave?' Not a single day passed without a tussle between Lizzy's thick tresses and her mother. Just when her mother began combing her hair, Lizzy would remember some work or the other. She would then struggle to break free like a bridled colt. Her mother was quite old fashioned. She had stepped into the house a young bride with big gold earrings dangling from her long earlobes, pierced and stretched, as was the custom then. Even now, her earlobes dangle all right, only there is no gold on them. It was her great desire to improve her daughter's looks by having her earlobes stretched as well. When no one in the family took her side in this matter, she looked upon it as a huge defeat, at first. She was not at all satisfied with the ear studs, the size of two tiny grains, which adorned Lizzy's ears. But when her co-sister, her husband's younger brother's wife, arrived with her ears looking just like Lizzy's, she was greatly relieved. In fact, the two small grains that shone on Lizzy's ears now looked modern.

Why, they look beautiful in our eyes too! They enhance her dusky complexion. But her eyes, black as beetles, are far more beautiful. What a multitude of expressions flash across those eyes! Just one look at those eyes is enough to testify to Lizzy's beauty. And when she smiles, there is no room for doubt in the matter. As for Lizzy, poor thing, she was oblivious to the fact that she went unnoticed simply because she had to compete with two rivals in the same house. One of them was, of course, her *Chithi*, her uncle's wife. Even after childbirth her Chithi remained fair and beautiful. The other was her Chithi's child who had inherited her mother's fair looks. The mother and child reminded Lizzy of a pair of roses on a single stem. How did these two beauties land in this small village? Should they come to Lizzy's house, of all places? It was on their account that Lizzy's beauty went unnoticed by others; why, even by her poor self. True, the villagers were ill-informed on many respects but they certainly knew the worth of a fair complexion. Lizzy too realized it whenever she cuddled her Chithi's child.

We said that the house was a large one, though old. The womenfolk knew their place in it. On no account did

Lizzy's Chithi come anywhere near the adichukootu. She stepped out only on Sundays when she visited the church. Even then, she had to come out through the back door and walk around the house without lifting her head until she crossed the adichukootu where her father-in-law sat. On the rare occasions when her Chithi went out, only Lizzy stood watching till she disappeared from sight. Whether or not her Chithi liked the clothes she wore, in Lizzy's eyes they seemed very elegant. Her Chithi kept her clothes neatly folded in a box. Sometimes when the clothes were taken out to be aired, the strong scent of naphthalene balls that rose along with the fragrance of talcum powder gave Lizzy such delight.

If Lizzy thought highly of her Chithi, her Chithi thought no less about herself. Chithi often wrote to her family. She had such good handwriting; each letter distinct and rounded like a pearl. It was Chithi who helped Lizzy with her math homework. Moreover, Chithi had some relatives in Thiruvananthapuram town—wonder what a town looked like! 'Weren't these enough to make Chithi proud?' thought Lizzy. Spurred by the desire to be like her Chithi, Lizzy started going to school. Only later did Lizzy realize that there were far more interesting things at school than her Chithi.

At first, her mother and father were reluctant to send her to school. Her mother couldn't bear to part with her beloved daughter. In any case, what was Lizzy going to accomplish by going to school, trudging nearly a mile everyday, she argued. Her father didn't know the value of education. He was aware, though, of the age-old refrain, 'Of what use to girls is education when all they do is tend the oven?' As it were, he was sad that his only child had turned out to be a girl. Worse still, he couldn't keep her in comfort. He took off for at least an hour everyday to the toddy shop to forget his sorrows. When he returned home reeking of toddy, he never dared go anywhere near the adichukootu. But from the way the old man spat hard, one knew he was aware that his dear son had returned home. Father and son never saw eye to eye. It had been ages since they had spoken to each other. Lizzy too mostly kept away from her father's bloodshot eyes and sought refuge with her grandfather.

Even in his drunken state, her father never grew noisy or quarrelsome. Somehow, he was an exception in this matter. Once he stepped into the house and stretched himself out in his room, he hardly stirred. The next morning, as Kannammai, her grandmother, remarked, he dragged his body like a beaten dog to the coffee stall. Only then did he feel revived. Then he dropped in on the leaseholders, hoping to collect some rent. After all, he was the son of a respectable family, wasn't he? So there was no necessity to earn a living. Besides, there was no enthusiasm left in him for any work these days. In truth, there was nothing at all to hold his interest.

The family grew used to this. Only the old woman's grumblings continued as ever. She had not grown tired of reproaching her son as yet. But it was of no use. The eldest daughter-in-law, the wretched woman married to this drunkard, had long since given up crying. Her husband had done nothing to make her feel proud of him. She directed all her affection, not to mention her anger, towards her only child. Lizzy found her mother's love very comforting. But at the same time, her anger and her restrictions were insufferable. Kannammai often took her mother's side. So Lizzy fled to the adichukootu. Only Kannammai had the right to follow her there.

'What is it child?' This was Kannapachi, her grandfather.

'...m.'

'What mischief did you do, eh?'

'*Amme* wants to beat me.'

'Why? What did you do?'

'...m.'

'Ask Amme to get back to her chores.'

Once Kannapachi gave his verdict there could be no appeal. Even Kannammai walked away muttering and never dared to raise her hand after that.

Lizzy had yet another supporter in the house. No, not her Chithi. It was her *Chithappa*, her father's younger brother. Chithi was 'cultured,' which meant that she never interfered unnecessarily in matters concerning another's child. Chithappa always treated Lizzy like his own child. He pampered Lizzy, who had been the only child in the family for many years. Occasionally, when he brought sweets for his child, Lizzy received a share too. Chithappa had scant respect for his brother. As for Chithi, she never opened her mouth in this regard. Years later, Lizzy wondered how it had been possible for a woman to have stayed so quiet. On the contrary, Chithappa expressed his opinions quite openly.

One day, Lizzy's father didn't return home even though it was very late. Lizzy was in the kitchen eating rice and fish kuzhambu with relish when her mother sighed deeply, 'There's no sign of your *Appan*. Who knows if he's lying in some ditch or pond?'

'Good riddance!' muttered the old woman who sat munching betel leaves.

Lizzy's stomach turned. She didn't fully comprehend what was being said. Something had happened to her Appan. Were *Ammai* and Kannammai worried or angry? If she told Kannapachi, he would merely spit with all his might and not say a word. The child couldn't take it any longer. She left her plate of rice and ran to her Chithappa. He was seated on a mat, holding a lighted beedi, savouring the thin wisps of beedi smoke that curled up in the faint glow of the lamp.

'Chithappa!'

'What Kutty!'

'...m...m'

'What is it? Tell me?'

'Hasn't come home yet!'

'Who?'

Lizzy couldn't control her tears. She knew very well that Chithappa was aware of what she was saying. Then why did he taunt her so? For a second Lizzy thought that she shouldn't reply, that she should simply run away. But it seemed her little heart would burst. She couldn't bear it. Unable to withhold herself any longer, she bit her lips and cried, 'Appan!' But she was shocked at her Chithappa's reply.

'Ha, ha, ha, ha!'

What! Was it really Chithappa who was laughing? Appan could be in danger and here was Chithappa, laughing. Tears rolled down her cheeks.

On hearing her son's loud cackle, his mother said, 'Have you gone mad? The poor girl comes running to you without eating a morsel and here you are laughing!'

Chithappa stopped laughing, got up and hugged the child who stood distraught with tears. He then shouted at his mother.

'A fine son you've begotten! Why don't you mollycoddle him with some more toddy? The drunken lout! I'm keeping quiet for the sake of these poor things. Otherwise I would have thrown him out of the house by the scruff of his neck.' He stroked his thick moustache.

Lizzy struggled free from her uncle's embrace. Tears and anger welled up within her.

'Chithappa! Some day you'll drink too,' she shouted angrily.

'Eh, Kutty?'

'Chithappa, you smoke beedi, don't you? Our teacher said smoking makes a person thirsty. And when you are thirsty, you will take to drinking toddy. You just wait and see. You spoke ill of my Appan, called him a drunkard, but you will turn out to be an even greater drunkard,' Lizzy screamed as if possessed. Her little body trembled.

Just then her father arrived in a drunken stupor, lurching

unsteadily. 'Appa,' cried Lizzy and ran to hug that pitiful figure. Her father blinked uncomprehendingly. Leaning against the wall for support, he shook her off and hurried to his room. The door slammed shut with a loud bang.

For a long time Lizzy lay whimpering on the floor. She didn't know when she fell asleep. When she woke, it was already day. She was lying on a reed mat. Chithappa must have lifted her up after she fell asleep and put her down on the mat.

3

The Sparrow

No matter what, there is such joy in going to school. Lizzy liked the small village school. Better still, she liked the *nelli* and guava trees that grew nearby. But more than anything, she loved the friendship she found there. At school there was no Appan reeking of toddy. No Ammai to constantly chide her. No stains of red betel juice that Kannammai spat all over the place.

Lizzy was proud to say that she went to school. Of the women in that household, who had ever seen a school? Neither her Ammai nor her Kannammai, except of course her Chithi. Lizzy was going to be a teacher when she grew up. Then all the freedom and glory denied even to her Chithi would be hers. She would take her little sister—her Chithi's child—to school as well. She often fancied herself walking to school in a new voile sari, wielding a cane.

The good soul who arranged for Lizzy's schooling was none other than Mary, the Mission House Akka. She was in the eighth standard. Their friendship had blossomed at the village pond. Mission House Akka was not from such a well-to-do family. Her father was the *Upadesiyar*—the village catechist. Her mother took up embroidering work to supplement the family's income. So, Mary enjoyed a lot of freedom. She came to Putham Veedu once in a while on her way to school to meet her little friend. She walked into the house boldly through the adichukootu. Lizzy's grandfather welcomed her graciously. Novelties such as coffee hadn't reached Putham Veedu yet. There was poverty; but, none went hungry. If nothing else, there was always plenty of *panamkizhangu, panampazham, nungu,* guavas and mangoes. Mary was astonished at all this. The old man greeted her with whatever was available in the house. Sometimes it was even a glass of *akkani,* fresh palmyra sap. Mary ate whatever was offered without the slightest guile and skipped into the house in search of her little friend. But the women at Putham Veedu didn't approve of Mary, a girl old enough to wear a half-sari, being allowed such freedom.

Nonetheless, Mary exercised a great influence at Putham Veedu. Lizzy's grandfather was a deacon at the church. He had to treat the Upadesiyar's daughter with respect. Moreover, who else was there to bring magazines and books for Chithi every now and then?

It was Mary who, a few years ago, had recommended that Lizzy be sent to school. As Chithappa was always there to support Lizzy and as Kannapachi was in favour of the idea too, Lizzy's side won. A slate and a pencil—bought from the village shop—came into her possession and Lizzy too became an honourable student.

Don't imagine, though, that Lizzy was granted special privileges on account of this. The way things were in that house it was just not possible to make any concessions, even for a child going to school. The school was a mile and a half away. Lizzy had to leave home at least by half past eight, so cooking rice as early as that, especially for her, was simply out of the question. Barring Lizzy's father, everyone, including Kannapachi and her little sister ate the previous day's leftovers in the morning. Lizzy too ate leftovers in the morning. But what was she to do for the afternoon? She had to take leftovers again. At least in the morning there was fish kuzhambu. But you couldn't take rice with fish kuzhambu to school. The other children would laugh. Mission House Akka had revealed this important secret to her. True, most of the children there ate fish. But if you had to eat fish in front of everyone, it must be fried. So, leftover rice and chutney were her only recourse. Here again, Lizzy learnt a trick. On no account must anyone know that it was leftover rice. In this way, Lizzy learnt many lessons, even before she had set foot in school.

She was quite clever in her studies as well. How else could she have passed four classes in five years? Considering her situation, it was no easy matter, was it? There was Chithi at home to help her, but then again, Chithi had her own child to look after. The very thought of her Chithi's child gladdened Lizzy's heart. She often pictured herself teaching her little sister. She would seat the little one on her lap once in a while, brandish a cane, teach her to repeat 'one', 'two', 'three' and pacify her when she started crying. She wondered when she could take her to school and let everyone see what a fine sister she had. Somehow, her mother's indifference towards her Chithi's child only deepened Lizzy's love for it.

One day, when she returned from school, Chithi greeted her with the child.

'Lizzy, we're going to name your sister.'

'What name?'

'What name? Why don't *you* suggest a name?'

'What do I know?'

'Don't the children studying in your class have beautiful names?'

'Oh, they do, they do.'

'Then suggest a nice, lovely name.'

'Nalini, Suganthi, Vimala... Emily! Emily sounds good, doesn't it, Chithi?'

'But it wouldn't rhyme with our Lizzy Kutty's name. Look, I thought of 'Lily'. How do you like it? Lizzy, Lily, Lizzy, Lily,' her Chithi said holding the child's chin.

Lizzy jumped up in joy. She was about to hug her Chithi but held herself back, feeling too shy all of a sudden. Instead, she seized the child from her Chithi's arms and kissed her till she began to cry. In just a matter of another two years, not just Lizzy but Lizzy and Lily would go to school. Lily in Lizzy's care. Lizzy rejoiced.

However, at school there was no time to think of Lily. Lizzy had an hour everyday at school to do as she pleased during the lunch interval. A good portion of it was spent eating the leftovers. Then she rushed to the only branch of the guava tree that arched downwards. If you didn't hurry you found no place left on the branch. Besides, only if you climbed onto the tip of the branch could you hope to swing up and down as on a see-saw. You also got to play the 'driver'. You could pick up and drop the little ones on the branch at all the bus stops from Trivandrum to Nagercoil. Lizzy liked the driver's job more than the conductor's. The conductor's seat was at the base of the branch. Perched there, you couldn't see-saw all that well. So, it wasn't much fun. Don't think that all the children on the guava tree were girls. In primary school, little boys and girls played together. Most of the boys were shirtless and girls with unkempt hair were a common sight. But such things never dampened the spirit of the game. Lizzy was treated with special respect in this group. Even though she was dressed poorly, the news that she was from a respectable family had reached the school even before her. It must have been the Mission House Akka's doing. Whatever the case, the children conferred a special status on her. Lizzy's boldness and daring were also partly responsible for this status. Only once did she lose that stature.

Lizzy heard someone tease her as she sat on the tip of the branch.

'Hey, *Aasaan*!'

Lizzy looked down.

The nickname—'teacher'—referred to her. There was no mistaking it. She knew the boy who had addressed her thus very well. It was none other than Thangaraj, the boy who had the hallowed privilege of always being at the bottom of the class. The children called him 'Rasa'. He was almost fourteen, grown up and full of pranks and mischief. There was not a day when he didn't get a taste of the teacher's cane. But Lizzy wasn't one to be cowed down easily, was she? Wasn't she bold enough to give a fitting reply?

'Le, *Mandoogam*—nitwit!'

A loud peal of laughter rose from the guava tree. It only proved that Lizzy's side was stronger. It was a unanimous approval of the nickname Lizzy had just yelled out.

In reply, Thangaraj picked up a handful of sand and pebbles and threw it on the speeding tree-bus. After all, how could a boy take such an insult lying down? Many of the passengers started rubbing their eyes. They searched angrily for Rasa. But was Rasa a nitwit to remain standing there after what had happened? At once, the children turned on Lizzy.

'*Kalli*—you culprit! Get down!'

'Look what happens if you are the driver.'

'We'll teach you a lesson.'

'Must tell the teacher, must tell her that she called him by a nickname.'

At the mention of the teacher, Lizzy remembered something. It was time for the bell. Before the bell, before

Rasa or anyone else, she must run to the teacher and report what had happened. Rubbing her eyes, she dashed towards the school gate and reached it in a trice.

Who knows what happened after that? When the children returned after the bell, Thangaraj was standing near the teacher's table with a vacant look on his face, while Lizzy was seated in the front bench blinking like the real culprit.

At four o' clock the last bell rang.

'Le, Rasa! Did it hurt?' asked a boy.

Thangaraj stretched out his hand, which he had kept hidden behind his back until then.

'Ayyo...!' Several children cried out. Tears welled up in Lizzy's eyes too. Everyone tried to console him in some way or the other. One fellow offered him two roasted tamarind seeds from the folds of his dress, 'Here, eat these.' A little girl handed him a *nellikai* she had saved. Lizzy moved away. Who cared about her now?

The next day, Thangaraj sat as usual on his bench—the last bench—in stately splendour. Lizzy felt guilty. Before the teacher arrived, she went up to him, crossed her forefingers and asked fearfully, 'Dei Rasa, still angry with me?'

There seemed to be no hatred in the way he looked at her.

'What for? I got caned for what I did,' he said casually. Lizzy's heart whimpered.

'Dei, you get beaten every other day because you can't learn your lessons. Here keep this. Keep it safe in your math book. That's how I got to do math well,' said the naive girl.

She was still a small child compared to him. He glanced at her and accepted what she gave him with a smile.

It was a peacock's feather. He wanted to laugh out loud but checked himself and put the 'present' carefully between the pages of his math book.

4

The Mission House

There is a small church in Panaivilai village where Christians attend the Sunday service. Many churches, full of passion and spiritual zeal at the beginning, turn lifeless as the fire dies out with the passage of time. This is one such church. Temporal concerns have pushed spirituality to the backseat. Some still attend the service out of habit. All the rituals surrounding weddings, funerals and baptisms continue to be performed here. The church receives a lot of money by way of contributions. Also, it offers an opportunity for the womenfolk to meet once in a while and exchange news. Though the Bible is read here every week, the church hasn't made much inroads into the lives of the people. Perhaps it is owing to the natural bounty of the place, which renders men neglectful of spiritual matters. Or is it their inherent apathy? Who knows? Like many other churches, it once had a primary school attached to it. But later when all primary schools were taken over by the government, the school shifted to a place nearly a mile and a half away. Only Sunday lessons are held in the old building nowadays.

We had said that the old man at Putham Veedu was one of the church elders. If at all he still remained the deacon, it was simply out of custom. The churchgoers, wishing to honour him, let him stay the deacon. Otherwise, he was in no way suitable for the post. The other deacons, in fact, looked down on him. But neither the Upadesiyar nor the parish wished to strip him of this honour. It was the general opinion that having somehow remained the deacon for so many years, he must not be troubled. He led the choir during the services too. His voice was never sweet and it didn't get any better with age. Nevertheless, the congregation joined in only after he began singing. And so, apart from the deacon's title, they had also willingly given him the position of the chorister. The power he had wielded in the village in the past seemed 'certificate' enough. The memory of his dominion still remained in everyone's heart, even though he was now old, wearied and baffled by the behaviour of his sons, his former wealth reduced to nothing.

It was not a surprise then that the church never progressed. If this was the case with the church elders, the Upadesiyar was no better. Mary's father, Moses, was the Upadesiyar. He never failed in his duties. In keeping with the old tradition, he visited the families of the parish and kept in touch with them. All the same, he lacked the power to attract the parish towards him or the church. Poor man, after all, he was a very ordinary person. What was the use of blaming him?

On Sundays, Lizzy sometimes accompanied her Kannapachi to the Mission House after the service. In the beginning, Lizzy never let go of her Kannapachi's hand. The Mission House always amazed her. It was a very small house! Quite old too! But well kept. No matter when she went, the floors appeared as if they had been scrubbed just then. You never saw a single housefly or their ilk. There were two or three pictures on the spotless white walls and a calendar too. There was a small cupboard full of magazines and books—English books too. A large Bible sat on the table. There was a Bible in Lizzy's house too. It belonged to Kannapachi and was as ancient-looking as him.

After she got to know Mary Akka, she usually ran to her, letting go of her Kannapachi's hand. *'Did Mary Akka stitch that table cover? Is it Mary Akka who is playing the harmonium? Who taught her? Will they teach me too? Will I be able to play it if I learnt?'* Such questions arose in her little heart.

Lizzy, however, didn't like the courtyard in the Mission House. They had cleared it and planted tapioca all over it. There was no room for Lizzy to run around as she pleased. Weren't her legs used to running around Putham Veedu, unmindful of the thorny thickets that grew there? Here you felt caged. How could Mary's brothers stay so quiet!

One day, Mary welcomed her with a mischievous smile. 'I have a present for you, look!'

Lizzy was not used to receiving presents. Her eyes widened in surprise. Mary went in and returned, holding aloft a birdcage. There was a mynah inside.

'For me?' asked Lizzy. Before she could go any nearer, Mary shouted 'Stop!' and shook the birdcage. 'Lizz...eee! Lizz...eee!' screeched the mynah.

Even before Lizzy got over her surprise, Mary said, 'I trained this bird for you. My brother, Rose, caught it. How is it? Do you like it?'

But Lizzy was thinking hard. She looked at Mary and pleaded, 'Akka, now that you have trained this bird to say my name will you teach it one more thing? It says "Lizzy, Lizzy" now. Can you make it say "Lily-Lizzy"?'

Mary's mother, who came there just then, laughed. 'Mary, know what? Her sister is going to be baptized this week. They've even handed over the name to your father. Seems they're going to call her "Lily". She thinks it would be a nice present for her sister, mischievous girl!'

Mary laughed too. 'Will you be getting a new skirt, then?'

'Of course! New skirt, silk jumper, ribbon, just like sister's, Chithappa bought it all for me.'

Mary's mother looked at her with pity and went back to the kitchen to do her chores.

On the whole, Lizzy liked the people at the Mission House. They treated her with such love, thought the child. Everyone at the Mission House, including Mary, was dark complexioned, as if oil had been rubbed into their skins. Subsisting on a meagre income, they didn't have the well-nourished appearance of the other villagers. Mary's mother was just skin and bones. Even so, Lizzy liked their way of living. In fact, she liked it very much. The way Mary and her mother treated each other, her fondness for her father—Lizzy couldn't think any further. How could she not shed a tear every time she stepped into Putham Veedu after visiting the Mission House?

5

Imprisonment

How swiftly the years fly by! How life changes utterly and irrevocably! How a child, who ran around freely, pelting stones at the fruits on the nelli tree, splashing about in the village pond, shouting, quarrelling and laughing with carefree abandon, is reduced, before long, to the wretchedness of peeping guiltily from behind doors, her face scarcely visible, the end of her half-sari tucked firmly around her waist lest it slips from her shoulders! Alas, such is life's strange play!

That half-hidden face we see from the adichukootu is none other than Lizzy's. Those eyes, they are unmistakably hers. They give her away. But they no longer sparkle with joy or mischief. Sadness haunts them. Or is it the shadow of a dream? Perhaps, it is just weariness. Who knows? She has oiled her hair well and braided it into two neat plaits.

Her face is oily too, haggard and careworn. There's no smile to brighten that dusky face. Is that Lizzy? Our Lizzy? Why does she look so crushed and humiliated?

First of all, you must understand that Lizzy belongs to a respectable family. If you have forgotten that, this is just the right time to recall it. As for Lizzy, on no account must she forget it. Never! She hails from a respectable family. The pride of Panaivilai Putham Veedu! So it doesn't become her to step out of the house and be seen by all and sundry. It will only bring down her worth. Secondly, confining young women to the house is an ancient Tamil custom. It was in vogue even during the Sangam age. Fortunately, this remains a secret. Not that people at Panaivilai Putham Veedu are familiar with the practices of the Sangam age. After all, they are no scholars of Tamil. Nevertheless, they are well aware of the customs handed down from generation to generation. Lizzy is now fourteen. She has come of age. She has taken to wearing the half-sari. So confining Lizzy to the house is of utmost importance. If you look at Lizzy's face, only her eyes seem to ask you 'Why? But why?' Now don't feel sad about this. For if you take this to heart, what will you do about the plight of countless other Tamil women?

No one cared in the least about the innumerable dreams Lizzy nurtured so lovingly in her heart. She was not a naive, helpless girl. At first she did throw a tantrum. Then she cried long and hard and remained stubborn. She protested quietly in every way she knew. But how long could a child hold out in the midst of such opposition? Forget Appan and Ammai.

Let them do as they please. But should even Kannapachi join their side? As for Kannammai, you needn't say anything about her. Couldn't Chithi at least have put in a word for her? As usual, she was forbidden to speak. Mary Akka was not in the village just then; she was in Palayamkottai, studying in some college. Mary Akka had her Chithappa, Mama and so many others to educate her. But who did poor Lizzy have?

Fine. They didn't send her to school. Couldn't they at least allow her to the church? She could at least meet a friend or two there. But Kannapachi was very firm. 'Where's the need for all that now? The two of them can go out together by and by. Besides, whoever heard of such things in our family?' he said with absolute finality.

Lizzy understood whom Kannapachi meant when he said 'two'. But she was more concerned about the present than the future. The hope that someday she and Lily could go out together was not at all comforting at the moment.

All said and done, the young cannot remain unhappy for long. That which is a bitter *ettikkai* at first, becomes simply a matter of habit in time. Life imparts worldly wisdom. So what if Lizzy didn't go to school? She had her house, didn't she? So what if she didn't have friends? There was Mary Akka's mynah. Lily, her beloved Lily, was there. Much of the day passed in petting and cuddling her sweet Lily. It was such a joy to have Lily's little head on her lap. As for the household chores, they were not all that burdensome. If it pleased her she did everything herself. Otherwise, weren't Ammai and Chithi there? After all, wasn't she the beloved

Imprisonment

child of a respectable family? Thus did the poor girl console herself over the course of time.

Moreover, why did she have to long for the privilege of going out, for prestige, position and such things? A great honour awaited her at home. Kannapachi's eyesight was weakening by the day. After Kannammai—it was almost two years now since her demise—Kannapachi felt increasingly lonely and disconsolate. He sought Lizzy's companionship more than ever. So it turned out that Lizzy was granted the privilege of coming to the adichukootu. Given the situation, there was no harm in it, was there? Besides, who else was there to read out the Bible and the newspaper to Kannapachi whenever he wanted? And so Lizzy acquired the privilege of moving proudly about the adichukootu, an honour denied even to her Ammai and Chithi. They couldn't even utter a word to their father-in-law. As for their husbands, they rarely spoke to their father. Even Chithappa seldom spoke to Kannapachi these days! Thus, Lizzy was Kannapachi's only help and support in that house. If anything, she knew that. As a result, she grew more affectionate towards the old man.

Things were no longer the same in the house. How everything had changed! Kannammai, who munched betel leaves all the time like a goat, was no more. Who was now there to look to Lizzy, hoping that she would pound the betel and nut? Still, the family depended on Lizzy for so many things. It was all Lizzy's doing. Lizzy had learnt a few lessons from Mary Akka's Mission House. She knew that her village house, unremarkable though it was, could still be kept clean. She made a separate place for the large heap of palmyra fruit and another for the palm kernels that Kannapachi chopped up for the cows. Thus she set the house in order. Nowadays, there weren't so many troublesome flies around. She even stitched a curtain for the window that opened out into the adichukootu. It proved to be very convenient for Lizzy. Occasionally, someone or the other dropped in to talk to Kannapachi. At such times, she could watch everything quietly from within the house.

Only now it looked like a house where womenfolk lived. Lizzy no longer admired her Chithi as she used to. Couldn't Chithi look after the house? All Chithi knew was to drape her sari well and powder her face daintily. After Kannammai passed away, she didn't even know how to get along with Lizzy's Ammai. These days there was a perpetual shadow of worry on Chithi's face. Chithappa often went to Trivandrum on business trips. Sometimes he brought home a relative. Wasn't that reason enough to keep the house clean? The rose bush that blossomed in the inner courtyard—how lovely the flowers looked! Just like Lily's soft cheeks, like Lizzy's forgotten dreams. Again, there was only Lizzy to care for it. Who else was there?

If Lizzy wasn't clever, could they have managed to retain her Appan in the house? True, they couldn't stop him from going to the toddy shop. But Lizzy had succeeded in keeping him away from the coffee stall. Why should he go to the hotel when the same delicacies were available at home? Like Kannapachi, he was also dependent on Lizzy, wasn't he? So

Imprisonment

there was something to make her proud and content. How else could you go on living?

What Lizzy liked best in this life of hers was the palmyra climbing season. Akkani was her favourite drink. She was never repelled by the flies and ants that lay dead in the akkani. She simply removed them with a ladle, dipped her cup into the pot and drank it. But that was not the only reason. During the akkani season, an old woman came home to boil it. Lizzy found it was a good pastime to chat with her. When she scoured the yard with a broomstick for dry leaves to build a fire, Lizzy walked along with her. It was, after all, their yard. So there were no restrictions in walking there. The old woman's son went up their palmyras to collect the akkani. He was called Thangaiyan. As per the custom of palmyra climbing, a day's akkani belonged to Thangaiyan. When it was Thangaiyan's turn, his young wife arrived to fetch the akkani. They had two children. Both often came running naked with their mother. It was these people who added some spice to Lizzy's otherwise dull life.

So what if her doors were shut against the outside world? Here, inside her own house, an entire world took shape just for her. The way the *panaiyeris*—the palmyra climbers—arrived tapping their pitchers noisily, the way they chopped down the palm spathes even as they teetered among the fronds, looking as if they were about to seize the sky, the gusto with which they shouted their wisecracks to one another—it was all very interesting. And the things they talked about atop the palms! Every bit of news—from the Travancore Palace secrets to Hitler's military campaigns—was touched upon. For Lizzy it was more or less like going to school. She was learning new lessons in her own backyard.

There was a reason for Lizzy's exceptional fondness for Thangaiyan's mother. The old woman was very clever at flattering people. The livelihood of her family depended on the people at Panaivilai Putham Veedu. Was it surprising then that she had a natural talent for sweet talk? Thangaiyan was a burly fellow who lacked such finesse. He didn't realize how important it was to speak ingratiatingly in order to succeed in life. Whereas the old woman had suffered enough and learnt life's lessons well. *Even a small portion of gruel is worthwhile; you must never forget the hand that feeds you*—steeped in such worldly wisdom, she naturally liked everyone at Putham Veedu. It was not surprising therefore that Lizzy, who was the light of that household, appeared a great beauty in her eyes. It was the old woman again who kept repeating to the women of the house that Lizzy was indeed beautiful. It was she who brought from the village shop the flashy bangles that tinkled on Lizzy's well-rounded hands. Wasn't she the one who took the palm jaggery of that house to be sold in the market? Pethi was probably not her real name. But that was how she was known at Putham Veedu. What would the people at Putham Veedu do without her? Who else was there to bring them all the village news from time to time?

One day, on returning from the market, Pethi hurried into the kitchen, a palm spathe overflowing with fish in her hand. She was excited by some news she had brought.

'Where is my *rasathi*?'

Rasathi was one of the many terms of endearment she had bestowed on Lizzy. It was the general opinion at Putham Veedu that being a respectable family, they were entitled to such gracious forms of address.

'What, Pethi?'

'Is my clever one tending the fire? Dear girl, give this old woman a mouthful of *kanji* water if there's any. Do you know whom I met today?'

'Who, Pethi?' Lizzy asked, as she rinsed a clay pot.

'Your friend, Mary! Remember her?'

Lizzy's mother, who was grinding spices intervened, 'Did this girl ever forget her? It was she who never even looked this way.'

Lizzy cut her short. 'As if you allowed me to meet her! Did you allow me to go there even once?' she complained.

Lizzy's father, who sat in the *thaazhvaram*, the verandah of the inner courtyard, shouted, 'What's that now? What's that donkey saying?'

When a man's voice reverberates so loudly and strongly through the house, it is only natural, isn't it, that other voices must grow quiet? But Lizzy knew her limits. Sensing that her father's anger hadn't gone out of bounds, she went and sat near the old woman who was drinking kanji. 'Pethi, tell me, what did she say? Did she ask about me?' she asked eagerly, her heart beating with excitement.

'Can she forget my rasathi? She said she'll be coming here.'

'When? When?'

'I have forgotten. In which month does she get her big vacation? Said some *ingilees* name. What does this old woman know?'

The way Pethi said 'English'! Lizzy wanted to laugh. 'So then Pethi, is Mary Akka coming during her long vacation? Has she come to the Mission House here? When is she returning?'

'Seems she has to leave tomorrow; said she wasn't keeping well. Seems she drank some hospital medicine. She came to consult the *Vaidyar* here.'

'Well, as if she will come to our house!' This was Chithi who was in the opposite kitchen.

'Who is that? Is that Mekkuthi Ammai? Amma, she said some of your relatives will be coming here for four or five days.' Lizzy's Chithi was often referred to as Mekkuthi Ammai or simply *Mekkuthiya*.

'Yes. My *Annan* and *Anni* are coming in the month of May. Their son and daughter are coming too.'

'Oh! I believe that Kutty is studying with Mary. It seems she's Mary's friend.'

'Never mind all that. What fish did you buy for me?'

'Oh, *Kuthipu* for you. Five for four annas. It is time for the rains, isn't it? So Kuthipu has arrived. My rasathi Lizzyamma! Here, take these Nethili fish; you said there were raw mangoes in the house. You wanted Nethili, didn't you, to be cooked with the mangoes?' She washed her hands, took out all the fish from the basket and divided them into two lots.

Imprisonment

Catching the smell of fish, Lizzy's beloved cat came running, 'Miaow...miaow.' Have the mynah and cat ever been friends? As soon as it heard the cat, the mynah flapped its wings in fear and screeched, 'Lizzy! Lily! Lizzy! Lily!' instead of 'Lily! Lizzy!'

Again Lizzy's father's loud voice, 'What's that now? The lesson sounds all wrong?'

Lizzy laughed. 'No Appa, it's frightened. So it has forgotten its lesson.'

Just then a nine-year-old girl came skipping in with her book satchel. Lizzy went and took her bag. The little girl, Lizzy's dear Lily, hugged her. She didn't even mind that Lizzy reeked of fish just then.

6

The Palmyra Climbing Season

In the month of *Maargazhi,* a new fervour spills into the lives of the people in Panaivilai. It is the time when palmyra climbing happens in full swing. One sees signs of it everywhere. In the evening, the mothers and wives of the panaiyeris return from the market with their palm leaf *thondis.* If you happen to look into the thondis you'll find more than half of them filled with fish of every kind. There is a certain kind of fish—*Kilathi,* also known endearingly as *Manipass.* You can smell it even eight miles away. The sight of it is enough to send these women into a frenzy of excitement, evident in their lively gait and their noisy, animated chatter. It is also noticeable in their dusky, resplendent cheeks. Their new saris proclaim that their financial condition is satisfactory, at least in this season. The womenfolk of the panaiyeris do not know how to drape a sari in the modern way. They only wear it as the women of this region used to in the past. They sport silver bracelets and anklets. They don't even spare their toes. They adorn them with different sorts of toe rings.

The excitement of the season doesn't stop with the bright clothes and sprightly bearing of these women. It touches several other aspects of the village life too. Temples receive large quantities of palm jaggery as offerings and many arrive to procure it in the auction. The Mohammedans who are into the jaggery business get busy. Work begins in full swing at the sugarcane mill situated nearly four or five miles away, where some of the young men in the village also find work.

There is even a sudden spurt in court cases during this season. Just imagine that! In the panaiyeri households, no sooner do a few coins roll in than there is talk of buying a bit of land or at least the empty plot adjoining their backyard. They go about making enquiries. Needless to say, there are conmen and tricksters just waiting to come to their aid. Isn't this also the season when toddy flows in plenty? There are scuffles. Sometimes fist blows and even murder! Expenses go up. Is it a surprise then that possessions and property change hands?

Need one describe the travails of the panaiyeris who stir up such a flurry of activity? They move about in the darkness of the night, clutching their pitchers under their armpits. If it is the first quarter of the moon, it may even be midnight by the time they reach home. During the last quarter, one hears the charak charak noises of the panaiyeris shinning up and down the palmyras, even as the first cock crows. The conference of the panaiyeris takes place atop the palms and many 'mumbers', as the panaiyeris are wont to say, take part in it. The sky is their meeting place. As for the work, it depends on each one's convenience. If Thangaiyan lets out a loud 'koo' from Putham Veedu, the panaiyeri who answers him with a 'koo' may be atop the lone palmyra within the Mission House compound nearly three or four palmyra fields away. Once they set the conversation rolling, those who partake of it may be anywhere within a radius of half a mile. Nature has bestowed such a unique privilege on them. During a good season, the conference proceeds in high spirits. How else can they get rid of all the energy in their bodies strengthened by the feast of tapioca and fat-rich fish?

Let us not imagine, though, that the panaiyeris don't have any hardships. They toil with their lives in their hands, such is their work. Not unlike that of the fisherfolk. A single spell of rain and there's trouble. The akkani that trickles and oozes all night in the pots that hang from the palms loses its consistency. It becomes unfit for boiling. If you take it to the toddy shops you may manage to sell it for a pittance. When thunder and lightning strike with noisy clamour, it needs a lot of grit to swing with the blustery winds at a height of seventy feet. If circumstances and practice have endowed the fisherfolk with courage, the same is true of the panaiyeris. How can a panaiyeri eke out his livelihood if he is scared of risks? Accidents do happen—one or two incidents every year. If there's a catastrophe at sea not even the body can be recovered. If there is a mishap from the top of a palm, you are sure to get the body, but it is no longer fit for anything. If you happen to visit the Neyyur hospital, you will get to see the condition of the panaiyeri who has had a fall. As for the plight of his wife and children, now that's another matter. Is palmyra climbing going to come to a standstill on account of all this?

What are the religious beliefs of the panaiyeris in Panaivilai village? It is not easy to answer this question. Falling in with the customs of the well-to-do families they work for, some either visit the London Mission Church or the mango-grove Kali temple close by. A few perform propitiatory rituals at home to appease the spirits. One or two families practice the art of black magic. Such practices are more or less on the wane though. In the midst of all this, there is even a Pentecost corner that resounds every now and then with loud music and fervent singing. Aren't so many religious groups enough for such a small village? Nonetheless, it must be said that the panaiyeris, by and large, aren't overwhelmed by religious sentiments. Religion is not the cog of life's wheel. If you ask the panaiyeri himself, he will tell you that his belly is his God. And that belly is dependent on the palmyra. Beyond this, his thoughts hardly dwell on spiritual matters. There is no point in scoffing at him for this; at least he speaks the truth. He certainly doesn't feign to be an enlightened soul. Mustn't we at least give him some respect for this? We are not venturing here to examine the religious doubts, fears and curiosities that may assail individuals. But one thing can be said for sure. There is no spate of religious fervour in Panaivilai. A majority of those who go to church just know that Christmas is the festival that celebrates the birth of Christ and that Christ was crucified on Good Friday. They know little else about Jesus Christ. The Bible lessons will enter their heads only if they listen, isn't it? This is more or less the state of the non-Christians too. They are familiar with the custom of wearing new clothes on the festival of Onam but hardly know why.

As regards literacy, they are not worried about such things. The older generation of panaiyeris was unlettered and gave hardly a thought to education. Nowadays, with the arrival of newspapers bearing interesting news stories, one or two have learnt to spell the letters of the alphabet and read for themselves. Some send their children regularly to school. A few others have their children studying in colleges. These latter ones have given rise to fumes of envious resentment in the neighbourhood. By and large, the panaiyeris stop their children from going to school at a very early age. They don't have enough money in their hands. Moreover, isn't palmyra climbing their ancestral vocation? Can they give it up?

Caste allegiance hasn't spared these panaiyeris. Compared to religious fervour, caste consciousness looms really large. Generally, the panaiyeris think highly of Mahatma Gandhi. But that has done little to mitigate their caste allegiance. Several other communities live in the village as minorities. Though the panaiyeris fraternize with them in every other way, they forbear from having any give and take with them in matters relating to matrimony.

The domestic life of the panaiyeris is just so-so. There are stray instances of a married panaiyeri consorting with another woman. Occasionally, you hear the story of a young girl eloping with a stranger. But these are exceptions. Though there are one or two love escapades and petty domestic quarrels, they abate quickly without affecting the grind of everyday life. The young girls are confined to their houses to some extent but the wives of the panaiyeris, by and large, enjoy considerable freedom.

It is said that even if you drink milk under the palmyra it will be mistaken for toddy. What, then, can be said of those who drink akkani atop the palms? Anyhow, it is akkani seasoned with plenty of lime. There is no alcohol in it. If it has to turn into toddy, the lime has to settle first. And then it must be left to ferment over a period of time. The panaiyeris do taste toddy every now and then. But it must be said that none of them drink in excess. They can't afford to. Once they shin up the palmyras they need to be alert till they come down. Toddy drinking is the exclusive privilege of the sons of affluent families. After all, they are ones who are without any other pastime.

'Koo! Koo!' The call was from the palmyra behind Putham Veedu.

'Koo! Koo! Thanagaiyaaa...! What is it, vei?' This was a panaiyeri from a palm tree in the compound of another big house nearby.

'Samikkanu! There are bugs up here. Such a menace!

Just now I slashed a frond down.'

'Koo! Koo!' This was from the palmyra in the mango-grove. 'Did you chop it down nicely?'

'Then what? Will I spare it?'

'Koo! Koo!' This was from the Mission House palmyra. The lone palm cried out, 'Thangaiyov...!'

'What is it brother, Manikam?'

'So, when are you leaving?'

'Who told you?'

Thangaiyan was leaving Putham Veedu following a verbal tussle with the old man of the house.

'Why do you bother about that, le? I learnt you're leaving. The place you are going to, perhaps it's better off there?' retorted Manikkam.

'There are probably no bugs and beetles there. Ha! Ha! Ha!' This was Samikkanu's wisecrack.

'If you are polite and proper, you can somehow scrape together a living wherever you are. Otherwise, where will you manage to hold down a job?' remarked Manikkam.

Though this was Manikkam's philosophical rumination, the underlying thought was: *All said and done, they are bigwigs. Where was the need for Thangaiyan to argue with them?* Thangaiyan knew it too. You could thrash out anything on top of the palms. But you had to be careful not to get in the way of the bigwigs who lived in the rambling houses beneath the palms. It only ruined your livelihood.

Chara chara. Thangaiyan climbed down the tree. The chara chara noise rose as the palm-fibre hoop that held his ankles together rubbed against the tree trunk while he shinned down. The akkani was in the pitcher secured to his back with a rope tied around his waist. He clambered down quickly and emptied it into the pot kept ready under the tree. His wife Ponnammal stood there silently. From the way she blew her nose, it appeared that she had been crying. Her old mother-in-law, Lizzy's beloved Pethi, stood nearby too, silently sweeping the dry leaves with a broomstick worn thin. Only the leaves rustled. Her already bent back now arched at ninety degrees. Clutching his pitcher, Thangaiyan left to shin the palmyras in the next thicket. Ponnammal left too, blowing her nose and wiping her eyes. Only the dry leaves continued to rustle under the broomstick.

'What, Pethi!' It was Lizzy. She approached the old woman from somewhere behind the trees where she had been standing all along. 'What's all this?'

'Ah! Is that you, daughter? Where were you standing? Heard what this cursed fellow said? I've told this son of a corpse, told him many times. Never argue with the ones who feed us, never! There are already two little ones in hand and one on the way. Where will he go now, dragging me along? Am I a young girl to trudge all those miles?'

'Why, Pethi? Must you go too? Why, you can stay with us, can't you?'

The old woman's eyes grew moist. 'Child, may you live well for asking me to stay here with you all. But my precious one, in another two years I'll be running seventy. Will I be able to work then? Even if it is just gruel, he has to feed me, doesn't he? Can I ask your Appan and Ammai? You'll leave this house sooner or later, may you live well. Who'll take care of me then?'

Lizzy knew the meaning of the old woman's words. She would get married and leave the house someday, wouldn't she? So she didn't persist with her question any further. Her life too had never been a bed of roses. Still, her young heart was troubled by the distress of this poor old woman.

She went into the house and learnt the full story. In her opinion, Kannapachi was a good man. But he was quick-tempered. Besides, he was racked by the loneliness of old age. Lizzy was his sole companion. Still, there were only a few things that he could talk to her about. Once he got someone to talk to, he didn't easily let go of the person. Even if a panaiyeri happened to walk by, it was as if a man who had been just moving his empty mouth, pretending to be chewing, had got hold of a handful of rice flakes. It was not as if he preferred to speak only of this or that. The price of the akkani pots, the difficulties in getting firewood, the quality of the fronds that were cut down for extracting fibre—if one dropped in to consult him even on these matters it gave him such solace. But what did youngsters like Thangaiyan know about such niceties. Thangaiyan was full of the brashness of youth to say nothing of his inherent dismissive nature. He belonged to the league which believed that you needn't bow and scrape to anyone as long as there was strength left in your body. It was no surprise then that the old man didn't like him. It so happened that the two crossed swords over a paltry issue concerning panamkizhangu. It rankled the old man. Eventually, the old man called Thangaiyan one day and issued a month's notice. It only showed the old man's meanness.

Lizzy didn't know about it as she had been in the kitchen at the time. Had she known, she would have at least put in a word for Pethi's sake. Now the floods were well over the head. It had been arranged that on Thangaiyan's departure, his distant relative, Anbaiyan, should take charge of the palms. To Lizzy, both Thangaiyan and Anbaiyan were the same. However, not just Lizzy, but even the other women in the house were unhappy that Pethi was leaving. Henceforth, who would go to the market? Who would fetch water from the village well? Who would bring them all the village gossip from time to time? There were such difficulties. Lizzy had another problem. Pethi's imminent departure somehow grieved her deeply, a grief that she could not even share with anyone else. Who was going to understand it? Would Ammai, Appan or Kannapachi understand? After all, Pethi was an old woman; even Lily would laugh. Telling them was as good as telling the mynah.

The day came when Thangaiyan had to leave the village he knew so well. Only the old woman turned up to take leave of everyone at Putham Veedu. Her son didn't set foot anywhere in that direction.

'Dear child, my precious daughter! I thought I'd get to see your wedding! But look what this accursed fellow has done! It's not just the old man he has let down. See what he has done to me,' she wailed, cursing her son.

'So what, we'll send you a marriage invitation.' It was Lizzy's Chithi who said this. Lizzy was not expected to reply.

But Lily chuckled. 'Why Pethi, will you totter all the way here with your stick if we send a card? When is Akka going to get married! Will you be around till then?' she teased.

Her mother silenced her. 'Keep quiet, Kutty!'

But the old woman didn't give in. 'I'll come. I'll come. Am I going to die before that? Send a card. You must send a card,' she told Lizzy's mother.

'Aaa… Fine. Why talk of that now? Isn't there still time for all that?' Lizzy's mother said for the sake of a reply.

The moment came when she had to take leave of Kannapachi. The old woman folded her palms and fell on her knees in obeisance. Kannapachi merely stared at Lizzy and muttered a dismissive '…m.'

It was through the adichukootu that the old woman walked out of the house. Tears rolled down her cheeks. Lizzy didn't cry. But her heart beat loudly. She stood watching at the doorstep till the old woman disappeared from sight. Was this life, then, she wondered. Anbaiyan came the next day. There were charak charak noises from the palm trees as usual.

'Poor fellow, very respectful,' approved Kannapachi. Lizzy wondered how long this would last.

7

A Measure of Rope

With Anbaiyan's arrival, there were many changes at Putham Veedu. Very soon it became apparent to them that Anbaiyan was a step above them in prosperity. When he set foot in Panaivilai Village he had bought a hut on five cents of ground. It was there that he moved in with his family. It was situated about a mile and a half from Putham Veedu. So, none of his womenfolk showed up at Putham Veedu. Just the same, rumours reached here that there were five sovereigns of gold on his mother's ears, not to mention the gold bangles on his wife's hands. So it was impossible to call them for domestic work. 'The times are bad,' muttered Kannapachi. *'It is well and good that those women don't come here,'* thought Lizzy's mother. There was even talk that Anbaiyan was going to buy fifty cents adjacent to Putham Veedu. It didn't augur well at all. From the way things went, who knew, he might even put up a palatial house there. Won't that undermine the pride of Putham Veedu? Such thoughts and anxieties tormented everyone in the house except the two children.

Kannapachi was in a very awkward situation, one he could neither spit nor swallow. Who could be blamed? After all, he was the one, wasn't he, who summoned Anbaiyan for the palmyra climbing? As for Anbaiyan, wasn't he polite and respectful, all said and done ? How could he be faulted? He was a panaiyeri. Barring that, what was amiss with him that he should he be deprived of a respectable status in the Nadar community? He kept to himself, his family and his work. A lean, strapping figure, a clean towel around his waist, a mop of black hair interwoven with strands of silver, brisk walk, efficient work—he was the picture of propriety. Though his face was dark, a winsome smile flashed across it every now and then. In Kannapachi's words, he was a fortunate man. But what could you do about it? It was said that he was a blessed man in his family life too. He had just two children, both sons. And he was going to build a palace for them to rule over!

'A fine panaiyeri our old man has got.' One morning, Lizzy's father, sitting in the thaazhvaaram of the inner courtyard embarked on a piece of analysis. It was said in a tone loud enough to reach the adichukootu.

'What of that now? He's going to buy a house, buy land. Were you able to do all this? You can't even see that you have a grown up daughter. He works hard. He thrives. Why carp at him?' Lizzy's mother countered him with unwonted rancour.

'Amma, please let it be!' This was Lizzy.

She never liked her Appan and Ammai bickering. What was more, Ammai's words were becoming increasingly fiery these days, especially at the sight of her. She rankled like a thorn in her mother's eyes or so it seemed to her.

'Let it be? Why should I let it be, Kutty? Who's going to carry you away? O that I had to bear you for a drunkard! Should I go to the streets and beg everyone, "please marry my daughter, marry her" uh?'

'Shut up, you cursed wretch!' Her father snapped back. 'Who knows which fellow is blessed enough to marry my daughter? You've a grudge against me. I've made a hag of you. But a fellow *will* come, you just wait. He'll look after your daughter like a princess. Why do you make her cry now?'

Lizzy was indeed crying. Only her tears assuaged her father's anger.

'So then the prince is coming to marry the princess!' Chithappa's loud voice rang from the adjacent room. 'Doesn't have the means to get her married to even a panaiyeri, seems he's going to send her to a palace! Did he get hold of the prince at a toddy shop, eh? As for the daughter, oh, she looks like a princess...lemon-skinned and lovely as a fig! Fellows are just waiting to pluck her away!'

By the time this spell of tongue-lashing came to an end, Lizzy was nowhere nearby. She sat on a wooden plank in the kitchen, sobbing. One of Chithappa's words stung her deeply. He had made it plain that she was dark, that there was no likelihood of her getting married without a suitable dowry. True, Lizzy was not like his daughter. Lily was not yet ten, but her beauty was already the talk of the village. Still... still, he needn't have rubbed it in. Was it really her Chithappa who had uttered those words? As a matter of fact, her Chithappa hadn't scoffed at her. But Lizzy didn't understand at that moment that it was her father he had jeered at.

Neither did her father realize that. Seething with anger, he got up and ran to the doorstep, ready to strike his brother.

'What did you say? You rascal! My child is in no way inferior to your girl, that white-skinned wretch! Who's going to marry my girl? You see for yourself! You just see!'

'Let me see. Let me see.' This time the retort was a decibel lower.

'As for you, what have *you* accomplished, uh? You keep going to Thiruvananthapuram twice a month. Are we better off for all that? Oh! There's plenty of money in the bank! Money! And your business is flourishing! Business! Ha, ha, ha, ha, ha!'

That laughter assailed Lizzy like a spear even as she sat in the kitchen. She stumbled up, ran to her father and held his hand. Alarmed that something was wrong, the mynah in the cage flapped its wings and screeched, 'Lizzy! Lily!' As Lizzy's father hurled the cage against the wall in a fit of rage, it forgot its lesson completely and cried frantically, 'Keech! Keech! Keech!'

A shadow fell across the threshold. It was Kannapachi. He stood there, clutching his stick. He shook with anger.

'What's happening there? You murderous fellows!'

Suddenly, the house grew quiet. Lizzy's father hung his head and walked out through the backyard.

'Thoo!'

Only Kannapachi could spit like that. It looked as if his spittle might even pierce the wall and hit the offender.

Thus, fumes of a new bitterness descended on the house that had never shown any sign of happiness. Moreover, Pethi's departure was a great loss to them. They were not in a position to hire anyone else for boiling the akkani. Going to the market, fetching water from the municipal well—for chores such as these they had to depend on a petulant girl. Not withstanding the three whole rupees they had to grudge her every month they were able say, 'Ei, Bhagyam! Fetch that here,' only with fear. What if she too stopped coming?

Chithi couldn't withstand the heat of the akkani oven. Lizzy's mother bought her portion of akkani too for a price and boiled it with her share. The fire from the akkani oven was not easy to bear. Consequently, Lizzy's mother appeared all the more dark, haggard and old. In her spare time she also had to scour the yard for dry leaves. As a result, Lizzy had to take on new responsibilities. In addition to shouldering all the work in the kitchen, it was she who had to place the akkani pot under the palms and carry it in once it was filled. Not that Lily was idle. She helped with what little chores she could manage. She swept the house and placed water for the milch goats. When she went to the village pond, she not only washed Lizzy's clothes but also carried home a small pot of water for her bath. She fed the mynah and the hens. What more could a little girl do? But it was not for nothing that she did all this. Didn't she walk gloriously to school everyday, carrying a box of hot rice and aviyal kootu and looking just like a little princess, her hair braided into two lovely plaits and adorned with rose, jasmine or oleander? Would all that have been possible without Lizzy?

Only the lives of the menfolk in the house progressed without any remarkable change. Kannapachi continued to snooze and spit. As usual, Lizzy's father passed his time drinking toddy. When sober, he spent his time either going around the village or sitting in the thaazhvaaram discussing others. Only Lizzy's Chithappa appeared busy. He travelled to Thiruvananthapuram very often. He had invested in a shop in the Chalai bazaar in Thiruvananthapuram. It was Kannapachi who had arranged for the money, pledging his entire property with a moneylender. There was talk that the business was sluggish. Consequently, Kannapachi was growing increasingly unhappy with his younger son. Also, someone had informed Kannapachi that his son had got into the habit of drinking brandy during his frequent trips to Thiruvananthapuram. If Kannapachi's younger son was at home there was some activity. There was a steady stream of visitors for him. The problems of the Travancore King, the fate of the British Empire, India's independence—such matters were thrashed out. At such times, their conferences took place in the adichukootu. Since his son did most of the talking, Kannapachi sat through it all with a grumpy face. That his words were simply passed over was his greatest grouse. Who came to visit him these days? At the most the Upadesiyar dropped in to pray, that too occasionally. Even Anbaiyan kept to himself and his work.

Anbaiyan had bought an acre of dry *punjai* land. He had paid five thousand in cash for it. He promptly secured it with a fence and planted tapioca in it. Surrounded by wild thickets of palmyra on all four sides, his piece of land looked invitingly green and irked others' eyes. He laid the stone foundation for a house in the middle of the plot. No, it was not the palace that had been expected. A small house, built of unfired clay bricks and thatched over with dried palm fronds. And in a matter of two weeks he would move into it. Everyone at Putham Veedu heaved a huge sigh of relief. A teeny-weeny house. There was not even money for a tiled roof. Every penny that Anbaiyan had in hand, practically his entire life's savings, had been shelled out. His mother and wife now went about with bare ears and hands. To that extent his fellow panaiyeris were satisfied. It must be said that Anbaiyan was yet to be accepted by his fellow panaiyeris. Wasn't he a newcomer, after all? It would be a while before mutual affection and kinship blossomed.

Anbaiyan's eldest son was not in Panaivilai. He had gone to Pondicherry for palmyra climbing. He would be back before they moved into the new house. The youngest son Chellappan was a still a boy, studying in school—the same school that Lily studied in. He was in the high school and was known to be clever at his studies. With mischievous eyes and not too dark skin, the boy looked handsome. Needless to say, Anbaiyan was very proud of him.

One afternoon, Anbaiyan stood hesitantly in front of the adichukootu of Putham Veedu with his son Chellappan. Kannapachi sat up on the bench, cast his failing eyesight in that direction, and peered hard.

'Who is it? Who's standing there?'

'It's me, Ayya.'

'Who is "me"?'

'It's me. Putham panaiyeri.'

'Oh, Anbaiyan? Come, come, what's the matter?'

'Nothing... it's just that we're shifting to our new house one of these days.'

'...m.'

'You must come to our house and give your blessings.'

The old man was flattered. 'When is the housewarming?'

'This Sunday evening. I've arranged with the Upadesiyar for a small prayer. You must come.'

'...m.'

'You mustn't refuse, Ayya. I'm depending on you. Let this poor man's dwelling prosper under your blessings.'

'Never mind all that, Anbaiya. All right, just call me when it's time.'

'My son will come. He'll be bringing the *Upadesi* and on the way, fetch you too.'

'Who? This mite of a fellow?'

'No! no! My eldest son. He's returning from Pondy tomorrow. After all, he has to take care of my affairs.'

The old man sighed deeply. He too had two sons. But what good were they, those wastrels?

'Fine. I'll come,' he said. Anbaiyan bowed and left.

Sunday afternoon. Lizzy was reading the Bible aloud to Kannapachi. She never read fluently. She only managed to stumble and stutter through it. And the two of them just about managed to surmise the general import of the verses.

A shadow fell across the threshold. Lizzy didn't know how long it had been there. But as soon as she sensed a man, a young man, standing there with the Upadesiyar, she sprang up, alerted her grandfather, 'Kannapachi, visitors!' and hastily went into the house without looking back. The Bible lay open on the bench. The pages fluttered noisily, as if to say they would fly away in the breeze. When she reached the doorstep, she stopped short and turned around instinctively on hearing a voice.

'Ah, is it you?' it cried.

She stared hard at the young man who had exclaimed thus. Yes. She had seen him somewhere. Suddenly, like a huge deluge, her memories rushed in. Wave after wave, they swirled over her and swept her away. For a minute she staggered, unable to bear their force. The happy memories of her childhood! The days when she flew around like a sparrow. The days when she was the '*aasaan*', the teacher. Yes. It was to him, this tall, fearless young man that she had one day given an excellent remedy from that precious little heart of hers, so that he would study well and understand math and escape the teacher's cane. This very same young man!

She couldn't bear it. She laughed aloud. Her laughter rippled like scattered pearls. It was laughter she had more or less forgotten. There was a lively sparkle in it. Never before had it resounded with such delight. You couldn't but turn your head and look, upon hearing it. It was the guileless laughter of a child. Was it really Lizzy who laughed? Had you seen her face at that moment it would have struck you that she was a great beauty. The joy that momentarily lit up her face like lightning also cast its glow on the young man's face, as he stood in front of her. He too laughed, perhaps recalling the past. Fortunately, Kannapachi's eyesight was not sharp enough.

But there were other eyes in the house, alert as an eagle's. Her own intuition told her that it was not proper to stand there any longer. As she hurried through the door, a rough arm caught hold of her right hand and pulled her in forcefully!

'Appan!'

'Who did you flash your smile at, you wretch! Do that again and I'll cut your head off!' They were just words. But coming as they did in a hushed tone through gritted teeth, they sounded like a snake's hiss to her.

It was only for a minute that she stood thinking. The next minute, deeply mortified, her face broke into a sweat. Her sister stood watching her without batting an eyelid. Who knew if Lily understood it all? What had her father said! How could he utter those words? He didn't say much, but there it was. Everything that had to be said had been said.

A Measure of Rope

For a girl like Lizzy, who had been confined to the house ever since she came of age and who had been brought up to revere feelings of honour and dishonour more than anything, what more was left of her maidenly life? How could she go on living after hearing this? Appa had pricked her with a thousand needles; pricked her and walked away, out of the house, so casually as if nothing had happened. He walked off to the toddy shop, where else?

She heard Kannapachi calling her loudly, 'Lizzy Amma! Fetch my things, dear!'

Trembling, she went into the room, took out the only *angavastram* laced with zari from the clothes chest, thrust it into Lily's hands and signalled to her. Lily ran to the adichukootu with it. Lizzy still stood at the doorstep, trembling. She heard the tap-tap of Kannapachi's walking stick. She locked herself inside the room and looked around.

It was pitch dark inside. It was a windowless room. But soon her eyes grew accustomed to the darkness. Clothes hung from a rope stretched across a corner of the room. Some white in colour, some with floral prints, a few old and frayed ones, torn ones, saris, new dhotis, Appan's shirts—it was a confused heap. Their clothes' chest was very small. It could hold a couple of clothes, that's all. She bent down and groped in a corner. A matchbox lay there—Appan's— for lighting beedi. She picked it up. What if she struck a matchstick and held it near the clothes?

It would all be over in five minutes. Yes. No one needed to know the anguish of her heart. She would die. All her troubles would come to an end.

She struck a match. Her hand shook as she held it and it burnt one of her fingers. The matchstick slipped from her fingers, fell on the floor and died out. She thrust her burnt finger into her mouth. She knew the taste of fire. Not once but several times had she sampled it while working in the kitchen. There had been occasions when she had spilled boiling kanji on her feet. A tiny speck of fire and how the body writhes in pain! What would happen if her entire body was on fire? Would she die quickly? Would it all be over soon? Curse it all! Who knew? Would it be a slow, torturous death? Blisters all over the body—the ears, nose, eyes, oh my God! This was not the way to die. Besides, these days they didn't let you die even if you wanted to. What if the smoke alerted them? Wouldn't they guess what was wrong and rush her to the Neyyur hospital just in time? She was dark, as it were. How would she look after that?

Suddenly, her heart forsook the clothes and leapt to the rope. Right. That was the right way. She snatched the rope and yanked it hard. It broke loose. The clothes fell in a heap on the floor. Lizzy knew how to make a noose. Once, a goat of hers had died as the rope around its neck had tightened into a noose. It would only take a minute. She ran her eyes over the ceiling, searching for a suitable spot to secure the rope. At the same time, her heart groped in the darkness. It was searching for something too. There it was—the first thing it discerned was her father's face. Drunkard! A depraved man! Prompt to judge his daughter. Did his daughter really commit a mistake? He didn't even venture to find out. What's more, it was he who was a great disgrace to the family! He deserved it. It would serve him right! Why did he need a daughter and a family? Her heart was bitter. Her eyes searched hurriedly. How could she reach the ceiling? There was no window. The clothes chest was not high enough. She flung the rope. It didn't reach the ceiling. It fell on the floor and lay like a snake in the darkness.

Her Ammai! She had no other succour. If Lizzy died, her only hold on life would go. Her grief-stricken Ammai rose in her mind's eye. How Ammai has changed! She has no strength left to even cry. She doesn't even have the energy to fully comprehend what it is to lose a dear one. She looks at her husband pitifully, with dull, vacant eyes. Behind her... yes, it is Kannapachi. Old and decrepit. He is searching for someone in the darkness like a child searching for its mother. Whom is he searching for, so frantically? Herself! It is her! Lizzie! Lizzyamma! Lizzy!

Can the faces in one's imagination possess so much power? And the voices in one's imagination, can they sound so disturbing? Her face broke into a sweat. Her knees weakened and she slumped down to the floor. Lizzy lost. Life, cruel life, cackled triumphantly. Tears welled in her eyes. She cried quietly. She cried till her heart's burden grew light.

Another face loomed through the tears. Hazy, indistinct, resplendent with youthfulness, love and desire. There! The semblance of the young man who was responsible for all this. No, this wouldn't do!

She wiped her tears with the end of her half-sari as though to efface the likeness of that young man and stood up. She had to accept defeat. Death doesn't come all that easily when man wants it. But... but... within those five minutes, Lizzy seemed to have died and been born again. Her tender heart, her child-like nature had turned to stone. She had to confront life, hadn't she? What was more, a new guile had entered her heart. She felt old and world-weary.

She had to resume her chores. The broken ends of the rope had to be secured again. She couldn't reach the bit still dangling from the wall. She left it all there, opened the door, and walked towards the adichukootu, relieved by the cool breeze that swept over her face, to see if Kannapachi had returned. He hadn't returned.

'Lily...!'

'What Akka?'

'Will you get me some rope?'

'You will find it in the cowshed. But why do you need a rope now?'

'Nothing, I broke the rope in that room. The wretched thing comes off even if you touch it. All the clothes were on it.'

8

The Relations from Town

'Lizzyamma!'

'What did you say, Kannapachi?'

'Just go in for a little while, child. That Upadesi fellow told me at the church today that he'd drop in sometime after noon. It's about time.'

'Why Kannapachi, he was here just last Sunday, wasn't he, on one of his usual rounds? What's so pressing now?'

'One or two things need to be discussed. That scoundrel—your Appan, is he at home?'

'Mm...Appa is at home.'

'Then you go ask your Appan to come here. Tell him the Upadesi will be coming now.'

Lizzy went in. The incident the other day had left a deep wound in her heart. She couldn't bring herself to talk to her father, face to face. She attended to him as usual. But in her heart of hearts, she stayed aloof. As for him, he didn't appear to have noticed it at all. He was perhaps a thoroughly insensitive being, who knew? He didn't even realize how he had broken his child's heart. He went to the toddy shop and came home as always, as if nothing had happened. He continued to address her affectionately.

'Appa, Kannapachi is calling.'

'What does the old man want?'

'Seems the Upadesiyar is coming now.'

'Let the Upadesi come first. Why should I go there now? I'll go after he comes. You go mind your chores, Kutty.'

Lizzy went to the kitchen. Her mother sat tending the akkani oven.

'Girl, go see what's happening there. I can hear your Appan-Chithappan's voices in the adichukootu. Looks like they're going to sell all the property and wipe us clean!'

'Why do you say that, Amma?'

'I know Kutty, the matter with your Appan and Chithappan. It's all your Chithi's doing. Wretched woman from Mekkuthi! All our possessions are going to pass into her hands, you just wait and watch! We're going to be left high and dry on the street. You go girl, find out what's happening there and tell me.

'Just don't say whatever comes to your mouth, Amma.'

'No Kutty, for sometime now, seeing the way your Chithappan and Chithi go about, speaking in hushed tones and the way your Appan and Chithappan are getting palsy-walsy and setting off to meet the Upadesi every now and then—your mother's stomach churns in fear. Go, just place a stool on this side of the window and be there. After all, who's there? Only your Appan, Chithappan and the Upadesi! If I come, the jaggery will get burnt. The *pathani* is already thick.'

Lizzy didn't have to be told again. Those in the adichukootu didn't notice the window curtain move.

Kannapachi and the Upadesiyar were seated on a bench. The Upadesiyar seemed a pillar of support. Between them lay Kannapachi's tattered and yellowed Bible and on it the Upadesiyar's beautiful leather bound one. What were the two doing there? The brothers had pulled up a bench right across and were seated on it. They remained aloof and looked as if they were sitting on thorns.

'So then, what's our say in the matter?' The Upadesiyar asked Kannapachi respectfully.

'What's there to ask me? These fellows have already decided everything, haven't they?' Kannapachi's voice was embittered. 'Anyway, there's no need to ask me anything. Nor will I come to the court for the registration.'

'In that case, what's left to speak about?' Lizzy's father was about to get up angrily. Chithappa caught hold of his right hand and made him sit.

'Wait, oi.' The Upadesiyar's voice rang with a little authority. 'Where are you going? You have a stake in the matter, don't you? Shouldn't you show some patience?'

'What, vei! The old fellow...no... Appan has made it clear once and for all. Then where's the talk of selling the land, eh? To whom? I don't have time for idle prattle.'

'Oh, yes, you've got work to attend to, so much back-breaking work. Work that's going to redeem the family!' Chithappa muttered derisively through his moustache.

'Don't we all know how well you have redeemed the family? It's you who have brought us to this state! How much debt do you have? Five thousand? Ten? That day, for your business, just to give his dearest son some money in cash, Appan pulled me along with him to the moneylender. Now when his granddaughter needs to be married off, he refuses to budge from the house. How's that?'

This last question was for the Upadesiyar. He looked at Kannapachi, who merely muttered a grim '...m.'

'Akka!'

This sweet voice was not from the adichukootu but sounded close to Lizzy.

'Sh...sh... Lily Kutty! Speak softly.'

'Akka! So then, it's sweet marriage for my precious Akka!'

'Go, Kutty! Who told you?'

'I heard Amma and Appa. Did you think I wouldn't understand? Isn't that what *Periyappa* and the others are discussing now?'

'Go Kutty, that's about selling the property.'

'Yes, why should they sell the property, Akka? Why, Akka? Akka Kutty, tell me!'

'Go Kutty! Wicked one! I'll cut your tongue.'

'Shall I fetch the knife, Akka? Why don't you cut my tongue?' said Lily. Making faces at Lizzy, she darted after a hen that had strayed in, shouting 'Ei, *kozhi*!' Her bangles tinkled as she ran.

The conversation was still on in the adichukootu; it was the Upadesiyar who spoke.

'Oi! Things won't come about if you're so impatient. Let me talk to *Ayya*. What, Ayya? Tell us what to do. What has happened has happened. Shouldn't we just move on now and see what's to be done next? There's a girl old enough to be married, there's debt to be settled.'

'And there are two overgrown sons...drunken louts!'

'What's the use of harping on that? Mustn't we now tend to the children whose lives lie ahead of them? Isn't that our duty?'

'Um.'

'Besides, there's no one to take care of all the property and holdings.'

'Why, what are these fellows for then?'

'There's no use in talking about that, is there? If you part with just five acres of your land, things can be settled!'

'Back in my day, would a fellow have dared to say this to my face? These are your times. But, do you know anything about my holdings, vei?'

'I know Ayya, a little. These two have told me that it's ancestral property and that you'll die of heartache if any of it passes into the hands of a stranger.'

'Oh! Then do these worthy fellows know even that?'

'Look Ayya, now suitable ways and means have risen just for that.'

'Suitable ways and means, ways and means!'

'No, I'm not joking Ayya. You needn't sell it to a stranger.'

'I'm not such a crazy nitwit. Aren't you talking about my younger daughter-in-law's brother? As if he's just waiting to row us ashore!'

'Don't worry about all that. Your younger son has convinced him and it's all more or less settled. You have to give your consent, that's all. Isn't that so, *Thambi*?'

The mustachioed man, Lizzy's Chithappa, nodded his head.

'Just five acres will do. Everything can be straightened out.' This was Lizzy's father.

'Things can be straightened out! Straightened out, it seems! What price will he give us?' Kannapachi asked his younger son face to face.

He mumbled with his head down. 'Ten thousand, half of it will suffice for the marriage.'

'Ten thousand? That panaiyeri fellow paid five for an acre. Doesn't this amount to merely two per acre? And for this property!'

'Isn't it, after all, ancestral property? It's not worth much.' Lizzy's father's voice grated like a saw.

'What did you say, Pilley?' Kannapachi staggered as he got up.

The Upadesiyar pacified him. 'What, oi! Is this the way to resolve matters? Shouldn't you have some respect for your Appan?' He reproached Lizzy's father.

'Why would he be like this if he knew all that?' said Kannapachi.

Anger flashed across the drunkard's eyes but he checked himself from saying anything.

'All right,' continued the Upadesiyar, 'Ayya listen, it's enough if you consent to give just five acres from that property next to your backyard. You needn't hesitate. We'd only feel more secure if decent people settle close by. My daughter Mary knows them all very well. The property will remain within the family. Our troubles would also come to an end. It will not cause the slightest impairment to Ayya's respectability. What Ayya? Is it okay with you then?'

'...'

'Just one word from you, Ayya. The future of this family depends on it.'

'...um.'

'Is it okay then, Ayya?'

'Oi! You've come all this way. These rascals have somehow dragged you here to back them up. Otherwise, will it all come through in this lifetime?'

'Then I am very happy. Shall I take leave, Ayya? I need to go to the Eastern house now for prayer. It's their turn.' The Upadesiyar stood up.

Lizzy's father followed him to the doorstep. 'Vei, Upadesi! Keep your sermons to the church. I'm not the one to be carried away by all that,' he seethed in a low voice and hastened in. Hanging his head down, the Upadesiyar walked out, looking sheepish.

By the time Lizzy's father crossed the adichukootu and reached the inner door, the stool was empty.

Lizzy came to her mother, 'I'll tell you later Amma, Appa is inside,' she said and went into the kitchen. She was soon busy cutting raw mangoes for pachadi. She tried to appear busy but her mind was thoroughly confused, like a muddied pond. Perhaps what Lily said was true. Would they arrange for her wedding as soon as the land was sold? Marriage might look like a pleasant affair at a distance. But when it was close at hand, several problems raised their heads. Who was the bridegroom? Who was going to tell her? If at all she came to know anything, it would be only through Lily. Lily probably knew very little at present. If she knew something, it wouldn't be a secret for much longer. As for her Appan and Chithappan, they seemed happy. Chithappa walked into his room, whistling. Unfurling a palm reed mat on the thaazhvaaram, Appa was happily getting ready for a snooze. Even Kannapachi had forgotten to spit. Poor Kannapachi! Lizzy didn't realize then that he actually sat dazed, thoroughly heartbroken to do anything.

Frantic preparations were on to welcome the relatives from town. Chithi washed the old, painted reed mats and hung them out to be dried in the sun. Chithappa borrowed the only cot and three chairs from the Mission House. Lizzy scrubbed the brass plates and tumblers that lay in a corner gathering dust with tamarind and turned them to gold. Even little Lily ran around busily, cleaning the house, dusting and swabbing the floor with cow dung.

The Relations from Town

The next morning, Lizzy's father went to the shop and bought a new sari for his wife and a finely woven pink half-sari with a matching silk blouse for his daughter.

'We should never let others know our plight, my daughter,' he said.

The curtain on the outer window was ripped down as it was tattered and a new floral printed curtain was put up instead. It occurred to none that it looked completely out of place with its surroundings.

Finally they arrived, the relatives. That tiny village lay just a little away from the thoroughfare. The blare of a horn or the noisy rattle of a speeding lorry was heard once in a while from the main road. But when had any vehicle, except perhaps a bullock cart, travelled down that eight feet mud track from the main road to Putham Veedu? So when a taxi pulled up at the doorstep with a loud pom-pom, everyone understood that the relatives from town had arrived. Chithappa and Lily dashed to the door. Even Appa hitched up his dhoti and followed them.

Four people got down from the taxi, entered the adichukootu and sat on the bench and chairs there. Two large, dark eyes observed them through the window curtain.

First came an elderly suit-clad man, more or less in his fifties. He ought to have known that this 'suit costume' would look ridiculous on his huge paunch. Had Lizzy been a child, just this would have been enough to tickle her to death.

Then came a middle-aged woman, not all that fair complexioned. But her sari was full of zari. Could it be worth a hundred rupees? Thin gold bangles adorned one of her hands, probably a dozen. But why wasn't she wearing any on the other? Were those slippers on her feet? What else?

But the girl who accompanied them—now she was surely a novelty! Her neck and hands were bare, simply bare. She wore a sari. From where had she managed to get such a flimsy one? The heels of her slippers were six inches high. For all that, was she beautiful? And Chithappa called Lizzy the dark one! Hadn't he ever seen this girl in Thiruvananthapuram?

When Lizzy saw the young man who came in last, her heart skipped a beat. Perhaps...no, no! Never! What was their status and where was poor Lizzy? When her family was relying on their help for her marriage would they deign to choose a bride from this house?

Still, she took a closer look at the young man. He sported sunglasses. How could he possibly see anything if he wore such dark glasses, she wondered. And with what insolence he carried his shoulder bag! Such arrogance!

As soon as Lizzy heard her Chithi's footsteps within the house, she quickly withdrew to the kitchen. Chithi, who had just returned after bathing in the pond, stood behind the main door drying her hair as she greeted everyone. 'Come in Anna, come in Anni! How John has grown! Did Elina write her exams well?' She took them in and laid out reed mats for them in the verandah along the inner courtyard. She brought them *achu murukku* and cashew sweets that had been prepared the previous day. After a great struggle, the two men who wore suits somehow managed to sit down in the verandah, their legs dangling into the courtyard. Lily, who kept to her mother, stood and walked with her, admiring the guests from every angle.

Who were those entering the house through the main door? Was it Mary Akka and her brother Rose? Just in time too. Must be Mary Akka. Lizzy, who stood observing them from the darkness of the kitchen, was startled in spite of herself. Though she recovered quickly and chided herself, she couldn't overcome her surprise.

Mary and Elina received each other as friends and conversed as equals. Mary looked fashionable too. She wore a wristwatch and had powdered her face up to the tip of her nose. She sat on the reed mat with her friend and chattered away gaily. As for Rose, he was in no way inferior to John in style. How casually he joined them in their prattle! And the smell of cigarettes! How it evoked the scent of towns!

What Lizzy found very, very surprising was the unreserved manner in which John, Mary, Rose and Elina, who were more or less of the same age, rubbed shoulders. However, nothing about their looks or conversation struck her eyes as unseemly or disagreeable. Lizzy's instinct told her that she would find no welcome in their midst. It was a different world. Lizzy had no place in it. Did she have no place in it at all? John's eyes fell on the old mynah.

'Adade! Look at this beauty! They have a cage for this bird, of all things!' he exclaimed.

'Is that what you think? Now look,' Mary laughed and gave the cage a little push. Poor creature, as usual it repeated its lesson, 'Lily Lizzy!'

'What do you say now?'

Everyone laughed.

'Not bad! I've never heard a bird talk before,' Elina's mother expressed her surprise.

'I caught this bird, do you know that? You're from the town. What can you possibly know about birds?' Rose said to John.

'Oh, come on now, that's enough! I trained this bird. Can he take greater credit than that, tell me?' That was Mary to John, of course.

Happiness, a flurry of excitement, then, a thousand other matters. Those who had been separated for a while were meeting again.

By the way, did Lizzy have no part in all this? No part at all? The one who gifted this mynah with such love and the one who looked after it like the apple of her eye—do they have nothing to share? Mary could have asked a word, just one word, about her old friend. Had she forgotten even that?

So what? This is the only way it could have ended; she had been just a child then. Such is the world. What was there to feel sad about? Nothing, nothing at all.

Lizzy stayed in the darkness of the kitchen, determined not to go in front of Mary until Mary herself came searching for her. After all, why should she go there, that too in front of those two young men? Lizzy didn't move from her place till Mary left.

Soon, Lizzy grew tired of the relations from town. She had to walk up and down the house for so many chores. After all, the guests were not strangers, reasoned her mother. Though Lizzy and her mother didn't appear to be strangers in the eyes of the visiting relatives, they probably looked like servants to them. Who knew? Very rarely did the two parties exchange words. Lizzy had no wish to consort with them. She had her pride. Never mind if they kept to themselves. It would be enough for her if that useless fellow in half-sleeved shirt stopped gaping at her when she walked up and down the house. Those eyes, they kept appearing in her heart now and then. She felt like punching them. Couldn't he at least wear those dark glasses?

Only then a thought struck her. Wasn't this fellow used to mingling freely with girls in town? Why, then, did he stare so hard at this village girl? Poor Lizzy, she did not realize how beautiful she looked in her simple clothes nor did it occur to her that it was her artless modesty that attracted him like a magnet. She kept aloof. He studied this wonder of all wonders speechlessly. It was all a novelty, a pastime for a young man from town; no more. As for her, she found it irritating beyond bearing.

It soon became apparent that these town folk couldn't stand the whiff of rustic life for long. Was there tap water here for them to bathe in as and when they pleased? There was not even an electric fan to assuage the heat when the temperature soared. There were not enough cots and no cotton mattresses on the existing ones either. There were so many drawbacks. Even Chithi was probably fed up with looking after her dear Anna and Anni. Chithappa, for his part, did all he could. He chopped down nungu for them. Bought visiris. But all that was not taken into account.

Meanwhile, talks were on. Everything was settled more or less satisfactorily. The Upadesiyar was also present when the matter was finalized. A day was fixed for the sale of the land and its registration.

Kannapachi came into the house and called Lizzy, 'Lizzyamma!'

'What Kannapachi?'

'Has Anbaiyan finished climbing the palms and left?'

'No, there he is, on that last palm.'

'Then tell him I sent for him when you go to fetch the akkani.'

Lizzy went out through the backdoor. Anbaiyan was shinning down the palm with great difficulty.

'Kannapachi is calling you.'

'I'm coming, daughter.'

Kiduk, kiduk. The noise rose from Anbaiyan's pitcher as he hurried to the adichukootu.

'Ayya, did you send for me?'

'Yes. We've to leave for the court registration early tomorrow morning. The journey is unsafe. I heard there's fear of dacoits over those parts. Is that so?'

'What can a dacoit do to us, Ayya?'

'No, it's the money. Not just a thousand or two, you see. I need a fellow or two to accompany us.'

'But it'll be almost ten by the time I finish climbing the palms.'

'Why don't you send your son? He isn't doing anything, is he?'

'He's into the tamarind business now, Ayya. A little buying and selling... That sort of thing. Doesn't matter, I'll send him. What else is he there for, if not to help you out in times of need?'

'That's why I asked! Ask him to fetch a bullock cart on his way.'

'At what time?'

'Eight o' clock in the morning.'

'Okay, Ayya.'

Kiduk, kiduk. He was a conscientious worker. Where did he have the time for further talk? He had to go home now and eat some leftovers.

The next morning, on hearing the jingle of the bullocks, the menfolk prepared to leave. When Lizzy fetched Kannapachi's things, she realized, instinctively, who the cheerful young man standing at the doorstep was. But, as they say, one smack of the whip is enough for the good bullock. Could she forget her father's words so easily? The truth was that he hadn't actually suspected her. Would he have spared her life had he really suspected something? He had merely warned her in his own fashion. Nonetheless, the lesson was deeply imprinted on her heart. She must not look at his face. Her Appan would kill her. The thought lay like a hardened stain in her heart.

As she walked into the house from the door without casting a single glance in his direction, she felt her heart beat with desire in spite of herself. He could have just said a word—like the other day—couldn't he? Who was going to take him to task? But, perhaps because he understood the situation or since she turned her face away, he didn't open his mouth. Lizzy went in.

As she walked in, she was thoroughly perplexed. Her father, probably, no longer suspected her. But she doubted herself now. Oh bother! What was this new distress! Why did the young man's face flash across her mind's eye ever so often? Her own heart as likely as not could be dissembling but one thing was certain, there was no guile whatsoever on his face. It reflected nothing but the unbidden joy that arises on seeing one's childhood friend. She made a resolution in her heart. She would never be the one to defile that pure, noble feeling of happiness. Never would she conduct herself, be it through her looks or speech, in a way that would cast the slightest shadow of contempt even in a corner of that young man's heart. That dignity, that respect, it was priceless. At least, let that last.

Her reflections were broken by voices outside. She took her usual place by the window. From there she would not be able to see him. But she could see Kannapachi and those around him.

'Why? Won't that Upadesi come today?' This was Kannapachi's query.

'Where's the need now? The matter has already been

agreed upon isn't it?' Chithappa replied glancing in the direction of the guests.

'All right, then count the money out and settle it, vei,' commanded Lizzy's father.

Chithi's brother signalled John who opened his shoulder bag and handed him a few bundles of cash from it. One, two, three, four, five bundles in all.

'Are they bundles of two thousands?' asked Kannapachi.

'No, only thousand.'

'Wasn't ten thousand the agreed sum?'

'Yes, ten thousand.'

'Where's the rest?' A shadow of doubt flitted across Kannapachi's face.

'What, Mama? Don't you trust me?'

'It's not that I don't trust you... But where's the money?'

'Yes, but you need only five right now to settle the debt, isn't that so? As for the rest, before the marriage I'll...' Lizzy's father didn't wait for him to complete. He sprang up, 'Vei, what are you saying? Better keep all the ten down.' He glared.

'I'm not talking to you, oi. I'm talking to your father. After all our own kith and kin, why would they doubt us, I thought, and decided to take the plunge. I'll be getting my provident fund money in another six months. If you insist, I'll sign a promissory note.'

'Vei, you and your note! Whom do you think you are pulling your tricks on? You're all town folk; you probably have a lawyer fellow in your hand. Besides, you yourself are employed in the court! Can we afford to fight you in the court, vei? What do you take us for, eh?'

The eldest son of the family ranted and raved in this fashion. Kannapachi simply blinked not knowing what to do. He looked pitiable. Lizzy's heart beat loudly. For a second, she didn't even recognize the shadow that fell across the threshold.

'Will you get your provident fund in six months then?' Kannapachi's voice was a mixture of disappointment and eagerness.

'Yes, till then shall I leave behind a thousand? For his satisfaction?' Chithi's brother nodded towards Lizzy's father.

'Your money and your filth! Come after six months, money in hand. We'll sign the deed.' The drunkard said firmly.

'Who'll come after six months, oi? What sort of kinship is this, without any trust? It's now or never. Are you the only one who can be stubborn?'

'No, not that we don't trust you...' Kannapachi drawled.

Just then a voice was heard. 'Ayya!' The shadow across the doorstep moved. Thangaraj approached Kannapachi respectfully.

'Ayya, shall I say a word?'

'What is it, Pilley?'

'I don't like this arrangement one bit.'

'Who are you, Pilley, to poke your nose in this?' Chithappa, who had remained silent all this while, shouted, his moustache trembling.

'I don't wish to come in between you kinfolk.'

'Then why do you interfere, I ask?'

The Relations from Town

'I can't bear to keep quiet after seeing Ayya's face.'

'Go see your Appan's face. Worthless panaiyeri fellow! If you stand here any longer...' Chithappa rose threateningly.

His brother sat there with a mischievous smile, delighted at the turn things were taking. Lizzy trembled. Thangaraj didn't move. His face had hardened to stone.

'What will you do?'

'I'll pound you and make mincemeat of you.' Chithappa ground his teeth.

'Why? What are my hands and legs for?'

'Sabash! Say that again, you brave fellow! Serves you right my brother, these words, that too from a panaiyeri fellow. Must beat your brains with a slipper! Brings his kinfolk all the way here, *his* kinfolk!' This was of course Lizzy's father. Whose words can sting so sharply. If anything, Appan knew how to taunt.

'Stop it!' Kannapachi's roar echoed unusually deep. 'He's fooling around, the scoundrel! Thangarasu, tell us what you wanted to say, Pilley.'

'If you ask me to leave, I'll go at once, Ayya. He made me almost forget I was standing before you.' Thangaraj said, looking at Lizzy's Chithappa.

'Never mind that, Pilley. What's your opinion in this matter?'

'Ayya, this is simply unfair. This property would easily fetch a quarter of a lakh. Besides, he says he'll pay a part of the sum later, all in good old trust. Did he at least mention a word about this earlier?'

Chithi's brother got up abruptly and looked at his wife., 'Susi! We don't have any business here any more. Every passing fellow has started interfering in the matter. Hm... come, let's leave,' he said in a tone of injured pride.

Helpless, Chithappa shook with anger. Appa and Kannapachi sat stupefied staring in different directions.

'Ayya!' Thangaraj continued, 'I'll bring people, Ayya. You can sell it for a quarter of a lakh. Even I can raise a five thousand, Ayya. I...'

'Stop it, Pilley!' the house shook as Kannapachi's voice rang through it. 'Be off, Pilley... go back to your house! I'm not selling my land. I'm not selling it to any fellow.'

'Who wants this fox-ridden wilderness?' Chithi's sister-in-law intervened. 'Did he listen when I told him? He came here carrying his suitcase, hoping his money would be of use to his sister's husband and daughter. Do you now understand the way your sister's people honour us all?' Her anger turned to tears.

Kannapachi only muttered a grim 'um.'

Thangaraj quietly slipped away from the place like a culprit.

The business of showing hospitality to the relatives from town ended in chaos.

They left in a fit of anger and commotion.

Lizzy sighed.

Kannapachi spat with all his might, 'Thoo!'

9

Lizzy-Lily

If a girl's marriage doesn't materialize for lack of money, will the wheel of time come to a standstill too? The world is indeed changing all around Panaivilai. The din over the freedom struggle has abated in the newspapers. The Travancore Tamil Nadu Congress struggle has taken its place instead. Electric poles now pierce the skies over Panaivilai too. There are even a few newly rich in the village. Tamarind business, jaggery business, building contracts—money flows in through different channels. Only Panaivilai Putham Veedu remains an exception to all this. Though the new house just behind it—Anbaiyan's house—hasn't changed much, it sports a new glory. There is a huge haystack in front of it. A haystack is more or less a sign of wealth and prosperity, isn't it?

Two beauties now adorn Panaivilai Putham Veedu. One

is Lizzy, of course; the other, her sister, Lily. Lily is now fifteen. She looks pretty in a half-sari. What wouldn't suit her lovely complexion, the delicate shade of screw pine flowers?

Lily was fortunate. Her studies didn't come to an abrupt end. It was only because she didn't clear her SSLC examination and because there was no money that she couldn't pursue her higher studies. Every time her father made a trip to Thiruvananthapuram, there were new clothes for her. Whether he incurred a profit or loss in his business, he at least ensured that his daughter didn't lack anything. She accompanied her mother to the church. She even had a Bible of her own—a small, beautiful Bible. She also went to the pond to bathe.

The reason for all this was that Kannapachi's stubborn say in matters had weakened. Lizzy's plight had turned out to be a terrible heartache to him, so he now preferred to keep quiet, not wishing to interfere in Lily's matter. Nevertheless, he muttered to himself that times had changed. When he spat in disgust, it was sometimes in disapproval of Lily too. All things considered, his affection for Lizzy only deepened. He worried whether he would get to see his beloved granddaughter's wedding in his lifetime.

Lizzy silently bore the changes wrought by time. When she saw her dear sister's life, she resented all the good things she had been denied. Nevertheless, having stayed within the house all these days, she thought it would be shameless to venture out all of a sudden like a brazen hussy. These days, the two sisters took some care to dress up. Fine silk and

Lizzy-Lily

talcum powder stood out in Lily's make-up. As for Lizzy, the jasmine and rose she nurtured so lovingly were her greatest adornments. Lily looked attractive, like a tender banana shoot, whereas Lizzy seemed a typical village girl. Alas, even the smile that was the distinctive mark of her beauty had lost its sparkle.

There was frequent talk of Lizzy's marriage at Putham Veedu. A girl, who was heir to property worth a quarter of a lakh, would certainly find a bridegroom, was her father's contention. But, those who come with proposal of marriage would expect cash in hand, wouldn't they? There was not a grain of gold on her hands or neck. Only a pair of red earrings. Even that had been made at her mother's insistence. As for her mother, she now looked shrunken and wasted, an image of spiteful resentment. Her husband called her the cursed old hag and, given the way she now behaved, it only seemed apt. Even Chithi was a shadow of her former self. Barring the days when he went to Thiruvananthapuram, Chithappa launched into a daily tirade against his father for not helping him settle his debts.

Although Lizzy worried about her future, wondering when things would start looking up for her, it was not as if she was completely bereft of hope. Over the past six or seven years, whenever talk of Lizzy's marriage came up, the thought of Thangaraj unfailingly rose in her heart. Would the bridegroom be like him, or would he turn out to be like the menfolk of her house—her Appan and Chithappan. She shuddered at the very thought of it. Who knew what her destiny was? Her mother too had been a young girl like her. Though Lizzy hadn't studied in any big school, life had taught her a lesson very well. It had etched the image of an ideal man deeply in her heart.

When he went past Putham Veedu, Thangaraj never once glanced at Lizzy. His instincts told him that any attempt to revive his childhood friendship with her—a girl from a reputed family—would be highly improper. As a matter of fact, it was *her* conduct, which caused him to think this way. Getting familiar with her would only tarnish her reputation. He was not an insensitive young man who didn't understand that. Besides, he was not someone who wished to see others suffer on his account. Why should he befriend her? Were they going to give her in marriage to him? Poor girl, a drunken lout from some big family would probably take her away. Who knew? He might be invited for wedding or he might not be. What ties did a panaiyeri's son have there?

There were times when he was engrossed in thoughts of her without being aware of it. But as a rule, he never spoke of the people at Putham Veedu in his house. When the news of his intervention in the property matter had reached Anbaiyan's ears, he had gone home and scolded his son.

'What do you think, Pilley? It's a matter concerning the bigwigs. What business does a cur have in a cottonseed store, eh? If they get together, will they spare you, Pilley? I struggle to eke out a livelihood with some respectability. Are you out to ruin that?'

Thangaraj never forgot that lesson. Notwithstanding

that, Lizzy's Chithappa accosted him one day and gave him a mouthful, 'Ei, Champion! Come here. Let me catch you interfering in my family matters again. I'll show you who I am. Be off!' Although his young blood boiled, he somehow controlled himself and reached home. Only his mother knew of it. She cautioned him, 'Son, my precious one, don't interfere in their matters, they are bigwigs.'

There were moments when he laughed to himself thinking, 'If at all one marries, one must bring home a bride from such a family!' One day, when he was returning home from the market, a voice hailed him from the toddy shop, 'Pilley, Rasa!' He turned around. It was none other than Lizzy's father. 'Come in, join me,' he invited him. 'No sir, I've some urgent work,' he replied and walked away without turning back.

However, as days passed and as his prosperity grew, a foolish desire rose in his heart. When Anbaiyan ventured to look for a bride for his son, Thangaraj protested loudly, 'What's the big hurry now, Appa?'

One day his mother argued, 'This isn't right, Pilley. We have to get things done at the right time.'

'Won't you keep quiet, Amma! Why are you so anxious? Has your son grown so old that you're dying to get him married? Is that it, eh?' he teased her and sealed her mouth.

Not that he considered himself to be the hero of a love story. A small desire had germinated in the bottom of his heart and was now budding. That was all. On the whole, he had a good opinion of Lizzy. 'Poor thing, a respectable girl,' he thought. Added to that, he pitied her for being a drunkard's daughter. But, more than anything, he remembered how she had run inside the other day after laughing like that. It was her innocent, cheerful face that came to his mind whenever he thought of her. To him, she was beautiful. Only, no one seemed to be coming to take her away. Why shouldn't he try asking for her hand?

Why not? He knew the answer to that quite well. First of all, his Appan wouldn't consent. Appan was a meek creature who wished to lead an unobtrusive life. Though his hard earned money was dear to him, he would never go in search of trouble even if it meant property worth a quarter of a lakh. Once they forged a kinship with Putham Veedu could they hope to live peacefully in this world ever again?

Secondly, he also knew what sort of a welcome he would get in Lizzy's house. If he dared to ask for her hand, everyone from her Kannapachi to her Chithappa would be raring to cut his head off. But a doubt wriggled and squirmed in his heart; a foolish desire—'What would she say? What did she think?'

He knew that those who asked for a girl's hand generally never consulted her in the matter. After all, what could a girl say? That was the custom. Things may be different among the educated. He knew of the love stories so prevalent in the film world; had seen romance in the movies. But he would never wish to associate this girl with that kind of love. Had she laughed at him or spoken to him whenever he went past their house, he would have probably concluded that she was a well-to-do hussy. Had she ventured beyond that, he would have turned away in disgust. But perhaps it was the way she kept her distance from him, considering him as any other young man and not a worthless panaiyeri, which drew him to her. Even when he wasn't thinking along these lines just one thing bothered him. 'What would she think?' He made up his mind. First he had to know the answer to this question. Everything else could wait. He waited for the right moment.

But never did he imagine that such a moment would present itself so easily. One morning, as Anbaiyan woke up and rolled his mat, he called out to his wife, 'Ei, make me a glass of sukku kashayam, will you?'

'Why, what's the matter?' asked his wife, concerned as she hurriedly prepared a concoction of dry ginger.

Anbaiyan's stomach ache didn't get any better. Perhaps, it was the previous day's fish.

'Appan should go to the Vaidyar. I'll take care of the palmyra climbing,' said Thangaraj.

The Vaidyar enjoyed a good reputation but Anbaiyan's stomach ache didn't show any signs of abating. His legs staggered. Thangaraj took over his work. He had been climbing the palmyras for almost two weeks now. It was Lizzy who usually came to collect the akkani pot. But Lily stood watching somewhere nearby, almost always; if not, she accompanied her sister. Lizzy never seemed to take any notice of him standing under the palm at all. Was he just a panaiyeri in her eyes then? He prepared to nip his desire in the bud.

Whatever it was, he decided that he must talk to her.

The next day, he carried a small bundle in the folds of his dress. She came with Lily. When she bent down to lift the akkani pot, he asked, 'Do you want *keerai* seeds for your yard? I've brought some good keerai seeds.'

Lizzy looked up. The pot was still on the ground.

'What keerai?'

'Red ones. Nice large leaves.'

He gave her the packet. Lily stood there casually. But when Lizzy looked at him, her memories of him engulfed her and whether or not she understood anything, it became clear to her at once that he had come there just to talk to her. Her face broke into a cold sweat. She thrust the packet into Lily's hand, lifted the pot and hurried into the house. She walked quickly, turning her flushed face away from Thangaraj and even from Lily, who apparently didn't notice it. Lily was still a child, wasn't she? But Thangaraj saw it. He also understood. What more could he expect?

After that he was in a flutter. His instinct told him that this girl certainly wouldn't refuse to be his wife. She was a virtuous girl, very honourable too. What more could he say to her? If he persisted, she might even misunderstand him and spurn him. No, he must never give room for that. At an opportune moment, he must have a word with her father. Lost in such thoughts, he walked home. But he didn't have the courage to broach the subject. However, the seeds of his desire now burgeoned in his heart, unchecked. So much so that, whenever he saw Lizzy these days, he only thought of her as his wife-to-be. He had very nearly forgotten that she was a girl from a big family.

For about a week, he had no opportunity to talk to her. Then Sunday arrived, and Lizzy came alone this time to take the akkani pot. He shinned down the palmyra and cleared his throat as an overture to what he wanted to say. Lizzy raised her head at once, instinctively, and stared at him as if to say, 'What is it?' At the same time, it appeared that she was in a hurry to leave.

'That day I interfered unnecessarily in that property matter. Is your Kannapachi is still angry?'

'When was that? How many years have gone by? Who remembers all that now?'

'But I haven't forgotten it. I was very immature then. You all had to face such hardship because of it.'

'What hardship? It's nothing new to us, is it?'

'So then nobody is angry with me now?'

'What do you mean *nobody*?'

'I mean none of you.'

'Looks like Chithappa still has some grudge. No one else. As for Amma, it's a consolation to her that the property is still with us.'

'What about you sisters?'

'I don't think anything. In any case, what do I have to do with such matters?'

Looks like she wouldn't give up her family so easily, thought Thanagaraj. Oh! She was about to hastily pick up the pot!

'Just one more thing...'

'You must tell me quickly. Amma is waiting near the oven.'

'It can't be said so quickly.'

'What is it now?'

From her face, it didn't appear that she had realized what he was about to ask her. There was only the anxiety that she must hurry. He mustered all his courage. He didn't dare look at her face though. Confused, he stared at the moon as he spoke.

'There's something I have to ask your father. I need the daughter's permission for that. Don't you understand?'

Unable to bear the stillness of the moon, he turned towards her face. He was alarmed. Her face had turned ashen, as if she had seen a ghost

'What is it? Perhaps I've made a mistake. Just a word, one word is enough. Shouldn't I have asked you? Please… can't you at least tell me that?' he stammered.

'Aiyyayo! It's not that. Appan will kill me. He'll certainly kill me.'

'Is that all? I thought…' His face, his entire being brightened and he looked at her with a mischievous smile.

'Isn't that enough? Aiyyayo! What have I done? There, that Kutty is back from the church. Let me go, *Theivame!*' She lifted the pot to her waist all at once and hurried away looking ruffled.

Thangaraj stood leaning against the palm, watching her. How long he stood there, no one knew. His heart was overwhelmed by a tumult of feelings, indescribable tenderness, joy and anxiety.

As Lizzy ascended the steps, Lily confronted her.

'Akka, go wash your face.'

What sort of a greeting was this? Lizzy placed the pot inside and came out silently. Lily bent down to pick up a jug of water and gave it to her.

'You don't even seem to remember that you need water to wash your face.'

Her voice bristled with anger. Lizzy took the jug and splashed the water over her face. How soothing it felt.

'Akka, your face is all flustered.'

True. Even Lily seemed to have noticed.

'Akka, everyone is going to ask you what the matter is.'

Her voice was unwavering. Not the slightest quiver! Was this Lily? Was this the little Lily she had cuddled and petted so lovingly? A shadow of suspicion seemed to be spreading across Lily's eyes?

'What did you say, Lily?'

'I know, Akka. There, look over there.'

He was still standing there. Oh bother! Wouldn't he let her live with some honour?

She couldn't bring herself to look at Lily's face, let alone say a word. Was she a culprit then? What crime had she committed? She couldn't come up with a convincing reply! What's more, she was not even able to quell the pricks of her own conscience! How was she going to prevail upon this wretch of a girl who stood unmoved, like hardened stone?

'If Appa or Periyappa come to know of it...'

'...'

'...they won't even spare your bones.'

'...'

'Kannapachi will die if he learns of it.'

'Lily! My precious Lily Kutty! How do you have the heart to tell Kannapachi? Besides, what have I done? Did I go talk to him on my own? Did you think that?'

'Akka, who said you were to blame? It was him I was talking about. Look at his eyes! Brought keerai seeds the other day! As if you asked him!'

'Shh... Lily! Speak softly. It's so embarrassing.'

'Won't it be embarrassing if they all come to know of it? Akka, they'll break his legs. He won't even be able to climb the palms after that.'

'What do you want now? Do you want to tell Kannapachi?'

'It all depends on how you conduct yourself.'

'My conduct? What do you mean? A great policewoman you are! You're out to find things, aren't you? When you went to school did anyone come snooping behind you?'

'Even if someone had come snooping what could they have found out?'

'What have you found out now, tell me? Why do you embarrass me like this?'

She felt as if her heart would burst in anguish. Seeing tears in her eyes, Lily felt confused. Still, she didn't relent.

'Akka, I've told you... I'll not tell anyone now. I had a strong suspicion. Whatever it is, you must never give room for such a thing, Akka. Let me not see him talking to you again! And that's final.'

'You suspected me, did you, Kutty? Who do you think I am? A slut? And you are the virtuous one. Is that so? Why do you then call me "Akka"? And what do you mean "that's final"? Look, I too have something to say. If you want to call me "Akka" respect me as your Akka. But if you think I am a slut, just stick to your policing. You needn't call me "Akka" anymore. You needn't! You needn't!'

Unable to bear it all, Lizzy burst into tears. Lily was distressed to see her cry. Tears welled up in her eyes too. She took hold of her sister's hand and was about to console her. 'Akka, my precious Akka…' but Lizzy shook her hand away angrily and wiped her eyes with the end of her sari. Lily was infuriated.

'Yes, Akka, I've told you once and for all. Just try talking to him again,' she threatened.

'Haven't you already said that?' Lizzy said angrily and went in taking the jug with her.

The first thing that her eyes fell on was the empty birdcage. Every time she saw it, it wrenched her heart, like a cradle that lies empty long after a child has passed away. She couldn't bear to see it now. It was several years since that mynah which called out 'Lily! Lizzy!' in a child's voice had become a thing of the past, a part of her fond memories of her childhood. Why then was that accursed cage still hanging there, tormenting her? She carried it into her father's room and left it in a dark corner. It stirred another memory. Yes, it was there, in that very same corner that the rope had fallen in a coil, a symbol of her defeat. It was a permanent defeat.

She was still floundering, caught in life's cruel grip.

Whether or not Thangaraj understood anything, he sensed that there was some misunderstanding between the sisters. He crept away from the place, his heart pounding loudly. For the next four or five days, he was in a flap, dreading that things might take an ugly turn at Putham Veedu. But nothing happened. Gradually, as days passed, his fear gave way to a sense of fulfilment. He had learnt what had to be learnt. The rest of it could be dealt with as and when circumstances arose. In the meantime, he realized that it was risky to speak to Lizzy. However hard he wracked his brain, there seemed to be no way he could take matters forward. Meanwhile, his father regained his strength and resumed palmyra climbing. Thangaraj attended to his tamarind business as before, that is, he made an effort to attend to it.

Was there someone other than his family to whom he could bare his soul? But confiding in someone, just like that, could prove to be disastrous. He had to approach someone who had some influence over the people at Putham Veedu. That the newcomers at the Mission House didn't have much rapport with Putham Veedu was a secret known to the entire village. After the old Upadesi left on transfer, Lizzy's grandfather lost his deacon status. Now he rarely visited the church, saying he was too old. Only his younger daughter-in-law went to the church as usual, taking Lily along with her.

As for Upadesis, they come in different breeds. It was said that the present Upadesi was a very learned man. But one rarely saw him anywhere other than the church. There were no ties whatsoever between him and the parish. Had it been the Upadesi who just left on transfer, things would have been different. He was a loving, God-fearing man; quite brave and eager to help. Thangaraj could have asked him for advice without the slightest mortification. It was the misfortune of the parish that he had to be sent away with a cursory farewell even before he could complete his term. He was averse to approaching the present Upadesi. But there was no other way. It had to be done.

After drinking his morning coffee, the Upadesiyar came out and sat in the verandah of the Mission House. His two-year-old child stood nearby, hugging his knees. Noticing a young man standing in the courtyard, he cried out, 'What, oi! What do you want?'

'Sir, I came to see you.'

'Come, sit down…' The Upadesiyar pointed to a chair close by. He looked Thangaraj up and down. From his appearance it was apparent that his financial position was quite satisfactory. And barring his robust physique there was nothing to show that he was just a panaiyeri. How could anyone not treat him with respect?

'What is the matter, oi?' he urged.

'I need a favour…' Thangaraj drawled, in his native tone. His speech gave him away. He was just an unlettered bumpkin or little better than that.

'You must put in a word for me at Putham Veedu.'

'Who are you? First, tell me that.'

'Thangaraj. I'm from your parish—the house to the east of Putham Veedu.'

'Oh! What do you do for a living?'

'Palmyra climbing. There's some tamarind business too.'

'Mm... What do you want now?'

'You must prevail upon the elder at Putham Veedu to give his granddaughter in marriage to me.' He blurted it out.

'This is a difficult matter, oi! You live next to them, don't you?'

'Yes.'

'Then you could very well ask him yourself, couldn't you? Or else why don't you ask your Appan to approach them?'

'That's not possible, sir. That's why I came to you.'

'That's nice, oi! Then do you expect me to ask them?'

'Sir, you are our preacher. Won't they listen if you speak to them?'

'I don't run such errands, oi. I've other work to do. By the way, it's that formerly well-to-do family, isn't it? The old man was one of the church deacons... It's his family, isn't it? He has two sons. Am I right?'

'Yes, those drunkards.'

'Why should I get into trouble, oi? You seem to know them quite well. I'm not even acquainted with them. Leave me out of this, oi.'

'Things may work out if you intercede, sir.' If Thangaraj were to give up now there was no other way out, was there?

'Sir, all said and done, their family and mine—we are of

the same community, aren't we? I've a respectable livelihood. There's some money in hand and I happen to own a few grounds of land. Moreover, they have grown weary of finding a suitor. Only there's none to intercede on my behalf.'

'Don't you understand, oi? You may be of the same community but you are from different subsects. Can't you see that when it comes to customs you are so different? If there's mutual liking, even the community doesn't matter. But in this case, there seems to be no amicability whatsoever between your families. I'm new to this place. What's the use of asking me, oi?'

It was pointless to stand there any longer. His entreaties were of no avail and he was overcome by a terrible sense of humiliation.

'Then I'll take leave, sir.'

He climbed down the steps and walked out, hanging his head down. The hope in his heart lay shattered like glass. There was no use in telling his father. His son's desire would mean nothing to him compared to his own fears. Approaching the people at Putham Veedu straightaway would only worsen matters. Had it been two or three weeks earlier, he would have repressed his desire but now it was beyond his power. Moreover, what would she think? Having got in the way of a naive, helpless girl who kept to herself, having asked her a question no one would ever dare ask a respectable girl, and having kindled her desires and hopes, he now stood a useless, gutless coward, who couldn't even open his mouth to utter a word. He was full of self-reproach. He had no strength left even for the usual playful, light-hearted jibes at his brother Chellappan.

'Why, Pilley! Why do you look do glum?' This was his Appan's query.

His grandmother, who sat before the akkani oven, remarked, 'A dog or a ghost must have assailed the fellow in the dark, who knows?'

'A ghost assailed him it seems, a ghost! His Appan should know better. He should've got him married in time!' Her daughter-in-law, Thangaraj's mother, was quick to observe.

'That's the only thing that's lacking now,' muttered Thangaraj.

'Yes, tired of quarrelling with her mother-in-law, she's eager for a daughter-in-law now,' Anbaiyan teased his wife.

Chellappan chuckled at once. But Thangaraj sat with a long face.

This was more or less Lizzy's plight too. Even after her worst fears were over, there was no peace in her heart. At times she was furious with Thangaraj. Why did he confuse matters! He had somehow managed to make her say and think things she should never have said or thought of. And what happened after that? He simply kept quiet. Was it all just a prank then? What did he take her for? While on the one hand he infuriated her, he also stirred up so many pleasant thoughts that she simply couldn't quell. He respected her heart. He respected her wish, something that neither her parents nor her Kannapachi had ever done. He loved her with all his heart, but he sought her approval. His eyes reflected

Lizzy-Lily

his respect for her feelings. Just that one thing was enough to gladden her heart.

But again the question arose. Why was he silent? Was he being merely playful? She was certain about one thing, however. Whether or not Thangaraj was fooling around, never again would she speak to Lily. Did Lily think she was clever? Educated? Beautiful? What did she care? What did it matter to Lizzy?

The cousins stopped speaking to each other. Their mothers surmised that something was amiss but were hardly worried about it. As a matter of fact, Lizzy's mother was pleased. Only Lily was a little hurt. But then, she too got over it soon and went back to being normal. As for Lizzy, she knew things would never be the same again. Her heart had hardened to stone.

Even so, she was thoroughly shaken by the news that Chithi brought back from the church one day. Her father was not at home. Her mother was scouring for dry leaves under the tamarind tree for the akkani oven. Lily walked behind her mother looking somber. She went in to change her clothes, when Lizzy heard her Chithi speak to Chithappa.

'Look here, there's a matter.'

'Mm...tell me.'

'I'll tell you if you promise to stay calm.'

'What do you mean I should stay calm? Never mind, tell me.'

'That Thangaraj fellow has asked for our Lizzy's hand.'

'What? Who told you that? Who allowed him to enter the house?'

'Not in our house. The Upadesi's house.'

'Did he go the Upadesi to find a way out? After all we paved the way for it didn't we, calling in the Upadesi to resolve our matters? Ei, the entire village is going to mock at us. Who told you this?'

'The Upadesi's wife.'

'Now she'll trumpet it to the entire village.'

Chithappa got up abruptly and went out to the backyard. Lizzy felt as if her heart would stop. Lily, who came out after changing her clothes, glared at Lizzy.

'You acted as if you knew nothing?'

'...'

'You wouldn't even speak to me, because I found fault with you.'

'...'

'What happened now?'

'What happened? It's as you wished. Appa will come to know. Kannapachi will learn of it. There will be a scuffle, then murder. You can see it all and rejoice. Why don't you also tell them something for your part?'

Chithappa was shouting in the backyard.

'Anbaiya! Keep your son inside your house, or else send him to Pondy. I don't know what will happen if he stays here.'

'Ayya, what are you saying? I don't understand!'

'Are you asking me what the matter is? Call your son. You ask him yourself. Has he hoodwinked you or what?'

'He has gone to his shop.'

'Did he go to the shop or to the Mission House? Seems he wants a bride. That's what he wants, a bride!'

Anbaiyan suspected that the man was drunk. Nevertheless, he replied politely, 'Ayya, let him come. I'll break his teeth.'

'If you don't do it, I'll break his teeth myself,' shouted Lily's father angrily and left.

Nothing happened at home as Lizzy had feared. Lily never opened her mouth, for Lizzy's words were deeply imprinted in her heart.

Until then, she had been sorry for her sister's distress but now she treated her with utter indifference. Her eyes called Lizzy 'a deceiver' without the slightest remorse. Thank God, the news didn't seem to have reached Lizzy's father or Kannapachi. At first, Lizzy didn't understand why Chithappa remained silent. Only later it became clear to her. His stern eyes followed her wherever she went. He had only to find out something suspicious about her conduct and then an earthquake would rip the house apart. She had to be very careful. What if Lily gave her away? Lizzy was wrought with anxiety.

When Thangaraj returned home, Anbaiyan recounted what had happened. Thangaraj remained silent. For the first time, doubt flitted across Anbaiyan's heart.

'What is it, Pilley? Are you dumb?'

'...'

'Whose hand did you ask for?'

'Which of the girls is old enough to be married in that house?'

'Wretched fellow! To whom did you ask?'

'...'

'Did you go to the Mission house?'

Anbaiyan sat with his hands over his head. He broke into a sweat. He called his wife and his mother to listen to the story of his son's heroic deed. Thangaraj was beset by loud wailing and angry protests. No one ate a morsel that day except Chellappan. Unable to bear his hunger, he drained a little kanji that lay neglected in the clay pot on the oven and drank some of it to quell the cruel pangs of his stomach. The fine seer fish that was in another pot remained untouched. He simply didn't have the heart to taste it.

10

The Illness and the Cure

Thangaraj went back to Pondy as before. His parents begged and beseeched him, berated him severely and somehow managed to send him away. Having no other choice, he left. His heart overflowed with bitterness. The very thought of the so-called 'respectable' filled him with intense loathing and disgust. He was partly angry with his father too. Why did his father have to be so chicken-hearted? Why did he have to call himself a man? As a matter of fact, that drunken lout from Putham Veedu—the younger one— who swaggered around twirling his moustache, seemed better than his father. He was even pluckier than Thangaraj himself. Wasn't Thangaraj now scuttling away like a beaten dog that runs for its life, its tail between its legs? What sort of a life was this? When all was said and done, what had been his crime? He merely wished to marry a girl from a reputable family. Let them judge if he was a suitable groom. Who was forbidding them? Why did they have to treat his father with such disregard? Which century did they think they were living in? If this was the kind of harassment meted out to a stranger like him, one could just imagine what they would do to their own girl.

Poor thing, the very thought of her plight wrung his heart. What if someone came to know that she had spoken to him? Did it matter? From now on, there could be nothing between them. Lizzy would be married off to some fellow or the other without any further delay. Could he even think of her after that? But would his heart pay heed? How loudly it protested even now! Somehow, he had nurtured this desire secretly in his heart. Now, to his great consternation, it loomed large, threatening to overwhelm him. Still, the young do not accept defeat all that easily. Things would come to pass, he hoped. In these twenty-eight years, time had wrought so many changes in his life. Hadn't there been days in his childhood when he had lain curled against his mother, holding his little stomach, unable to bear the pangs of hunger? Who could foresee the things to come? Come what may, he would have to face it. Such thoughts afflicted him.

As for Lizzy, a pleasant sense of exhilaration coursed through her heart. Thangaraj hadn't been playing around. It was only out of true love that he had gone to the Mission House to seek help. He could not be held responsible for what had happened after that. When a huge boulder comes rolling can a small clod stop its course? What did the pride and respectability of Putham Veedu matter when confronted with the longings of a young man? Hadn't she also seen so many of her desires crushed in her life? Who could be blamed for all this? It was her destiny! Lizzy had lost all hopes that Thangaraj's dreams would materialize. Nevertheless, it was comforting to know that he loved her with all his heart. He had conducted himself with compassion and forthrightness. Just that thought gave her the strength to get on with her life.

Through all this, a small doubt rankled her—had he sought her for her property? The doubt had risen of its own. No one had planted it in her heart. After all, was there anyone, anyone at all, who shared the secrets of her heart? One minute it pricked her heart like a thorn. The next minute she plucked it out. But it kept surfacing in some corner of her heart or the other. The hope that there were a few noble, decent people still left in this world was her only succour. What would she do if that hope snapped as well? So she nurtured her hope carefully in her heart. It was kept alive by her memories of Thangaraj. These days she didn't even consider it improper to think of him. Her only anxiety was that she somehow guard her secret. Only now she realized what it meant to be the heir to a huge property. It had always been and it continued to be a great hindrance to her joy. She started despising and cursing it with all her heart.

The very same property soon turned into a source of great anxiety at Putham Veedu. Though there was frequent talk of her Chithappa's debt, not once did it occur to them that it would affect everyone. If Kannapachi knew it, he did nothing. He merely drifted in and out of sleep owing to his senility. As soon as he ate something, he let out a loud belch and settled down with his visiri to ward off the flies. One could see flies hovering over Kannapachi's face all the time. Then when he felt sleepy, he simply curled his legs and fell into a slumber. It was only to Lizzy that he spoke with some love and affection. Even that was an occasional word or two. When he spat these days, it was not with malice or bitterness. Lizzy often wondered how old age reduced man to a pitiable figure. Kannapachi was no longer able to weave thondis and visiris from palm fronds. Even the palmyra fruit lay in a rotten heap under the trees with flies swarming all over them. Kannapachi had grown too old. The goings on in the world had no impact on him. He only ate and slept. Was there an Upadesi now, as of yore, to rouse him from his sleep?

A notice arrived from the court. Kannapachi was ordered to repay the money, interest and all—a huge amount—that he had borrowed for Chithappa by mortgaging his entire property. The repayment had to be done within three months, failing which they would lose their property. There would not even be a roof over their heads. They would have no sympathizers in the neighbourhood. Lizzy knew that. Bhagyam, who went to the market and bought things for them, had already hinted that she was going to quit. When the fig tree had been stripped clean of its fruits won't the birds know? The news had reached even Bhagyam's ears. Chithi and Lily seldom stepped out of the house, not wishing to see anyone. They didn't speak much to anyone in the house either. Chithappa was hardly at home. He was running here and there, frantically trying to raise the money. He even went to Thiruvananthapuram, to see his relatives. It seemed they were unable to help too.

One day, Lizzy's mother started wailing loudly, 'Kutty! If only your Appan was proper we wouldn't have to face such hardships. Even if we left this place we could somehow scrape out a living, climbing palms. What are we going to do now, my girl?' As for Kannapachi, he only felt sleepier than ever. Lizzy was not deeply affected by the distress of those around her. She had never enjoyed the luxuries of wealth nor had she experienced the torments of grinding poverty. So, unlike the others, she was not fraught with anxieties about the future. Nevertheless, it must be said that the distress of those around her helped her forget her own sorrows. As days passed, the court notice laid siege to the fortress of her heart and usurped even her memories of Thangaraj.

Lizzy's father drank harder than ever these days. One day, two burly panaiyeris had to carry him home from the toddy shop. They brought him through the adichukootu. Kannapachi, who was only half asleep, scarcely seemed to notice. But the way those fellows glanced at each other and smiled derisively! Lizzy, who had observed everything from behind the window, was mortified. She felt as if it was she who had been assaulted by their scornful looks and ridicule. After all, it was her father, her own flesh and blood! How could she stay unruffled? Her anger soon gave way to a flood of tears. She was racked by the memory of a similar incident from her childhood.

How could her father behave this way! And when he was sober, all he did was snigger, guffaw and taunt. Lizzy found his loud cackles intolerably offensive. One day, her mother got down to her usual nagging, 'Alas! Why did I have to bear a girl? Had it been a boy I wouldn't be the least bit afraid now.'

'Ei, accursed wretch! Why do you crib? Girl or boy, what difference does it make? Curse your luck!'

'Was it for nothing that the good Lord didn't give you a son? How lucky were you?'

'Oh! I wasn't fortunate enough. Certainly not as fortunate as my Appan! Ei, old hag, go ask that old man who lies in the adichukootu how much he owes the Lord to have fathered two sons. Hahaha! How fortunate he must have been. Ei, old hag! Have you fallen silent? Hahaha!' He burst into loud laughter at his own jibes. These days his jests and jibes only nauseated Lizzy.

It was many days since the two brothers had spoken to each other. The younger brother scurried away at the sight of his elder brother. Of late, the elder brother passed some remark or the other and laughed whenever he saw his younger brother. Only he could laugh like that.

'What, le! Seems your business is flourishing? Has your brother-in-law made arrangements for the money then? Did they extend warm hospitality?' Such were his questions. Fortunately, the younger brother merely glared in reply and walked away. Had he stopped to give a fitting reply, it would have ended in an ugly fracas.

To make matters worse, Kannapachi fell ill. He was completely bedridden. He coughed every now and then, but to Lizzy it seemed that it was sickness of the heart. If Kannapachi were to die now, in this condition, would her heart ever know peace? This sturdy man endowed with a large, robust physique, now lay before her eyes, wasted, like a banana shoot ripped to fibres! He lay in the adichukootu. He had his granddaughters to attend to him. Anbaiyan and his son Chellappan rendered whatever help they could, every now and then. Anbaiyan went about as if nothing had happened. Only Lily kept aloof whenever she saw him. She never looked at his face when she went to fetch the akkani pot. Lizzy was aggrieved that only Anbaiyan, this panaiyeri who was after all a stranger, came to assist Kannapachi and not either of his own sons. Appan came, peeped into the adichukootu and went away muttering an 'um.' Chithappa would occasionally sit for a while on a stool close by and then leave without saying a word. Kannapachi showed no signs of having noticed them at all.

Then the Vaidyar came. It was Anbaiyan who fetched him. Those at Putham Veedu had very few people whom they could call relatives in this world. Such was their fortune! At the turn of the twentieth century, cholera had struck down an entire branch of Kannapachi's brother's family. There were no ties whatsoever with even a few of their other distant relatives. There were one or two blood relatives in the neighbouring villages, but they lived in dire poverty. If at all they came to Putham Veedu, it was with the hope of taking something back home with them in their empty reed baskets. Consequently, they were only treated with the respect they merited. Thus there were none to help those at Putham Veedu in this situation. Only Anbaiyan ran to fetch the Vaidyar.

It had been nearly ten to twelve years since the Vaidyar had settled in that village. When he had first arrived in the village, he had merely accompanied his father, who was a quack. The old man passed away after procuring, with great difficulty, a government licence for medical practice for his only son. Meanwhile, the Vaidyar's fame spread all over the village. He even treated the sick in the neighbouring villages. Poor man, he didn't have the time to get married or even think of it, said the villagers. Being country folk, they had a strong faith in ancient *Siddha* medicine. Unless the Vaidyar himself advised them to take a patient to the local hospital, they rarely did so. They took great pride in him. It was he who treated Anbaiyan's family. Even Mary's father, the former Upadesi of the parish, used to consult him when someone or the other fell ill in his family. Needless to say, the Vaidyar was held in high esteem. He was reputed and rich. His elder sister was comfortably settled in Nagercoil with her children and her husband, who taught at a school. His two younger sisters—born several years after him—worked as teachers in a local school. Both were unmarried. Who was there to worry about such matters, remarked his mother to those who came to their house. Why would the Vaidyar, after all, shell out his money to get them married, ran the village gossip. Whatever it was, he was an expert at his work and the villagers respected him for that.

As soon as the Vaidyar arrived, Lily, who had been sitting next to Kannapachi, ran in to fetch her father. Hearing this, Lizzy came and sat behind the window curtain. Her heart beat with anxiety. Her father followed his brother into the adichukootu and greeted the Vaidyar with a gentle smile.

The Vaidyar held Kannapachi's long hand that lay limp in his right hand. He stretched and stroked the fingers as though he were tuning the strings of a veena. He rubbed the palm. Then he felt the pulse carefully with the fingers of his left hand. His large forehead creased and expanded.

Then, he took out a small packet from a little tin box between the folds of his clothes and gave it to Lily. 'Take a pill from this, powder it in an earthen pot, and mix it in hot water.' Lily ran in to powder it. Chithappa went out to buy medicines for the concoction. Lizzy's father sat talking hospitably to the Vaidyar. Lizzy noticed the Vaidyar's eyes rove here and there anxiously. He directed his gaze every now and then at the curtain, as if he expected to see someone. Lizzy withdrew hastily, feeling ashamed and frightened that the thin curtain may have given her away.

After that day, the Vaidyar dropped in daily. But Lizzy never picked up enough courage to sit behind the curtain. Kannapachi gradually regained his health. But his face was overcast by a shadow of anxiety.

One day, as soon as the Vaidyar had left after paying

his routine visit, Kannapachi called in a loud voice. 'Pilley! Ponnumuthu!'

Lizzy came running. How many days had it been since someone had called out her father's name in that house! What had happened to Kannapachi today?

'Appan is not at home, Kannapachi.'

'Lizzyamma, ask him to come here as soon as he returns. Don't forget!' he ordered.

When she informed her father, who came home to eat, he went to the adichukootu, muttering, 'the old man will neither die nor let anyone live in peace!' Finding his father's face unusually bright, he was a little taken aback.

'What's so pressing now?' he asked curtly and sat down next to him.

'Pilley, listen le, our child Lizzy is very fortunate.'

'Why, what's the matter?'

'The Vaidyar asked for her hand. You know their family, don't you?'

Lizzy's father didn't reply. He did know everything about the Vaidyar. But he doubted if the alliance would come through.

'We'll have to spend a fortune.'

'He says he's not interested in the money; seems he has plenty. He's even willing to lend us ten thousand rupees in cash to settle our debts; said that we can return it at our own convenience. He said we needn't worry about the jewels either; we only have to tell him and he'll get our child whatever jewels she wishes for. He said all we need to do is give him our girl without considering his age.' He rattled away and then paused to catch his breath.

'Our child has finally found a good match.'

'I told you so. It wasn't for nothing that she waited all these days! She's such a good-natured child. I knew, Pilley, that she'll fare well.'

Which father wouldn't be thrilled to hear his daughter being praised?

'Appan must wait. I'll go tell her mother.' He rose, and went towards the kitchen shouting, 'Ei, old hag!' in an unusually cheerful voice. He didn't even notice his beloved daughter standing behind the door. He was in such a flutter. Was it all true?

The Vaidyar went straight to his house, walked right up to the kitchen and called out, 'Amma!' His mother sat scraping coconut. Though she was almost sixty, she looked hale and hearty, a picture of good health. She wore a finely woven white cotton sari with a black border. Her hands and neck were bare but a lot of gold danged on her stretched ear lobes.

'What is it?'

'You needn't grumble henceforth. I've found a girl.'

'*Appada*! At last! Where did you find her?'

'Amma, that girl from Panaivilai Putham Veedu... Do you like her?'

His sister, who came and stood behind him remarked, 'I know her well, Anna! She's older than me. Must be twenty-two. Studied two classes ahead of me. By the way, Anna, what so special about her, um?'

Putham House

Her mother cut her short, 'Keep quiet, girl! When he has said he likes the girl there's no further ado about it; I like her too. Now what else, tell me,' she turned towards her son.

'No, Amma, I know that you won't refuse. I also knew that these two *kuttigal* won't like it one bit.' He looked at his sisters mischievously.

'Why do you say that?' Kamalam, the elder of the two sisters, retorted angrily.

'Kamalam, do you think she looks like us? She looks like a fair Brahmin girl. Doesn't she, Anna?' Kanakam, the younger one, asked him teasingly.

'Is there any doubt about it? You see for yourself,' he replied. The two girls started laughing. Before their laughter abated, his mother intervened, 'Which girl did you see? I know her well. She looks like your sisters. Perhaps you saw Lily, the younger son's daughter. Now, *she* is good-looking. Much younger too. I've seen her in the church. Why are you so quiet?'

Her son didn't say anything. Instead, he stood biting his lips. Kanakam laughed, clapping her hands. 'When has Annan ever noticed any girl properly?' Kamalam quipped.

'Confound it all! What's this new hassle?' muttered her brother.

'Why Anna, did you tell them anything?' asked Kamalam.

'That's the trouble now. I've already told her grandfather! What will he think now?'

Seeing her son's distress, the mother consoled him, 'Is this a big issue? You simply keep quiet. Just write a card to your brother-in-law and ask him to come down.'

But her son was full of self-reproach. 'This is really bad. What have I done?' he muttered, as he walked towards the portion of the house where the medicines were being ground.

There was much rejoicing at Panaivilai Putham Veedu. The house wore a festive look. Kannapachi was back on his feet. How could he lie down now? When Anbaiyan came to inquire after his health, he bragged, 'Anbaiya, there's going to be a wedding in the house. I don't care even if I die after that. Look at the child's good fortune.'

'So when is the bride-viewing ceremony?'

'Bride viewing? What bride viewing? Will such customs befit our family? Isn't it enough that we consent to give our girl? All said and done, she's going to take with her property worth a quarter of a lakh. Besides, what kind of a child is she? Can you find any fault with her?'

'When is the marriage?'

'Soon, very soon. Before this old man dies. Hahahaha!' he laughed like a child.

The two brothers went together and bought clothes for Lizzy, a thing that had never happened before. Wasn't she the bride now, after all? Everyone, including Bhagyam treated her with special respect. Even Chithi and Lily were jubilant that their debts were to be paid off and Lizzy's marriage was to take place, finally, as everyone had wished. But Lily still couldn't muster the courage to talk to her sister.

Their happiness gave Lizzy immense satisfaction. But she was not overjoyed. Instead, Thangaraj's image, which had grown faint and blurred over time, rose distinctly before her mind's eye. It talked to her, smiled at her and appeared in her dreams. It looked at her pitifully. She realized it was no longer proper to carry him thus in her heart. Still, he kept appearing before her. A great fortune had now come her way. At times, when she grew conscious of this, it seemed her heart would burst with pride. Despite this, there was no happiness in her heart. When she walked up and down the house, everyone merely thought that she looked comely, just like a bride. None of them paused to ask why there was no smile on her face. They only thought that she lacked nothing now.

A middle-aged man entered the adichukootu. 'From Nagercoil,' he introduced himself. Kannapachi understood at once. His sons guessed too. Need one mention the hustle and bustle that followed? They didn't even allow him to speak.

Finally, the visitor managed to hem and haw. 'Er... there's been a mistake. My brother-in-law is very upset.' He paused.

A heavy silence.

'My brother-in-law had actually seen your other girl, the younger one, he didn't know...'

Lily's father interrupted him. 'How is that possible? Can one give away the younger sister when the elder one remains unmarried? Is it proper? Besides, my girl is too young. She's still a playful child.'

'What can be done, oi? Somehow he has taken a liking to that girl. All these days he would neither hear nor let us speak of his marriage; now when he has expressed such a desire...'

'Desire! That shameless old fellow!' roared Lizzy's father as he stormed out. The visitor looked embarrassed. Kannapachi didn't open his mouth. It was his younger son who continued. 'This will only cause unnecessary resentment. There will be a big row in the family. Let's not talk about it. It's impossible. You may ask for Lizzy. There's no point in talking about anything else.'

'Then don't you need that ten thousand rupees?' The visitor held out the bait.

There was silence.

'My brother-in-law is willing to compromise so much for this girl. We want him to be happy, that's all. Once the marriage is over, he won't differentiate between his sisters and hers. Won't he do something for her too?'

'Never mind all that, oi, when there's a girl six to seven years her elder, can we...'

'After all, they are only cousins, aren't they, oi?'

Perplexed, the younger son looked at his father.

'What does Appan say?'

'Do as you wish. Why do you ask me?'

'We'll decide and let you know.'

The guest rose and took leave of them half-heartedly.

The news spread through the house like fire. Deeply mortified, Lizzy sat on a wooden plank in the darkness of the kitchen. She even forgot Thangaraj in that minute. She was angry and shaken, as if someone had outraged her in public.

Her mother went and stood behind one of the doors

that opened out into the adichukootu, all set for a quarrel. Her co-sister followed suit and took her position behind the other door. As if this was not enough, Lizzy's father strode into the adichukootu with fiery red eyes.

A storm raged.

No one heard Lily's loud sobs.

Lizzy didn't cry. Her eyes were dry.

Her father, who left the house that day, didn't show up anywhere in the area for the next two days. Till then, his wife and daughter didn't eat a morsel. They neither combed their hair nor swept the house. Anbaiyan sold the akkani and handed over the money to Lizzy's mother.

Lily's father was busy. Though he felt sorry for Lizzy, he was relieved that at least his troubles had somehow been resolved. And he was proud of his daughter. Besides, once the debts were settled, there would surely be some way out for Lizzy too. It was his wife who cheered him thus. She stopped speaking to her co-sister. Why invite trouble? It would only lead to a quarrel, wouldn't it?

A letter flew to Thiruvananthapuram. Swift came the reply. Soon, the marriage invitations were printed. The jewels arrived home in a beautiful box. The house was whitewashed. The ceremonial pandal was erected. The consent of the bride and the groom was officially announced in the church. There were just two days to go for the wedding. On Thursday morning, Ponnuthambi's daughter Lily and Vedamanikkam Vaidyar would be married at the Panaivilai church.

Kannapachi slept all the time. He had no worries

henceforth. The debts were settled. Even the document was signed and registered. It was enough if Lizzy gave her sister five thousand for her part sometime in the future. Then Lizzy's share of the property would be transferred to her name. But all this was in the distant future, after the days of the elders. At present, things would continue as they were before. Oh God, the trouble they had in coaxing Lizzy's father to go to the court for registration! Even Lizzy and her mother had to fall at his feet and implore him. What would become of the family if the debts were not settled?

The day before the marriage, the house overflowed with people—kith and kin, distant relatives, familiar and unfamiliar faces. The pandal was crowded too. So Lizzy made an effort to plait her hair and adorn it with flowers. She wore a new sari—of course the one her Chithappa had bought for her—and went about her chores as if nothing had happened. She was burning with shame. But she could not let others know this. The old women, who sat munching betel leaves inside the house, looked at her with pity. She didn't need their sympathy. It was beyond bearing. Lizzy fled to the kitchen.

Her father was not to be seen in the house at all. How could he bear to be there?

In the midst of so much confusion, those at Putham Veedu didn't notice that Thangaraj had returned. No one in his family could speak to him freely. The scowl on his face kept them at bay. Anbaiyan's only worry was that he might throw himself into a pit or a pond in a fit of desperation.

Lily's father searched for his brother. All said and done, it was an auspicious occasion, wasn't it? There was a crumbling mud wall behind Putham Veedu, just in front of Anbaiyan's house. A tamarind tree grew close by, its dense foliage overhanging the wall. The drunkard sat in its shade.

'Anna!' Lily's father called out his brother politely. He ought to address his brother respectfully at least on that day, oughtn't he?

The elder brother turned his bloodshot eyes in the direction of the voice.

'Anna, please come. Everyone is searching for you.'

'Be gone, Pilley! Keep off!'

Hearing voices at such proximity, Thangaraj came out of his house and stared. The younger brother who was already annoyed now grew incensed.

'Whom are you searching for? Who's waiting for you here?'

'It was *you* I looked at. Can't I even see who's talking in front of my house?'

'You can, you can. And you can also gawk at the girls inside respectable houses.'

Lizzy's father sprang up, 'What's this, Pilley? Why do you speak so rudely to him?'

'No, Anna. I never told you. This fellow had gone to the Mission House asking for your girl's hand.'

'What did you say?' Lizzy's father shook with anger.

Thangaraj intervened, 'What does it matter now?'

The younger brother laughed angrily, 'Do you ask how

it matters now? How dare you ask that after running away to Pondy and hiding there for six months? Just try showing your tricks again and I won't spare your head.'

'Is your head made of iron then?'

'What did you say?' The two brothers stepped forward angrily. Meanwhile, Anbaiyan who had set out to climb the palmyras came running hurriedly... Kiduk, kiduk, kiduk. He grabbed hold of his son's arm and pushed him aside.

'Wretched fellow! You've ruined everything! Ayya, why do you take any notice of him? I'll put some sense into his head. Crazy idiot! After all, a slip of a fellow... Must you get angry at him, Ayya?' He was almost on his knees, pleading. Thangaraj slunk back into the house.

'Be gone, Pilley, go do your work...you go too!' Lizzy's father commanded. Anbaiyan's father walked away, in a cold sweat... Kiduk kiduk. Having no choice, the bride's father slipped away too.

That night, Anbaiyan brought Chellappan with him to the marriage house to chop vegetables for the wedding feast. Lizzy's father didn't go to the toddy shop and instead sat slicing brinjals. At around midnight, Chellappan went all over the house searching for something. Could anyone hope to find a lost article in a marriage house?

The cock crowed the next morning. The air resounded with all the usual noises—the charak charak sounds of the panaiyeris shinning up the palms, the kiduk kiduk rattle of their pitchers and their loud voices calling out to those inside the houses to collect the akkani. Soft *nadaswara* music from a record player rose above these sounds. Arrangements had been made for the record player with a shop owner nearby. The air was spiked with the heady smell of rose, jasmine, sandal paste and bananas. A sweet fragrance wafted from the garland meant for welcoming the groom. Wrapped in a banana leaf, it was kept in the courtyard.

It is Lily's wedding. And she's crying.

'Poor thing, so tender-hearted! How will she bear the separation from her Ammai?'

'All said and done, he's twenty years her elder.'

'Poor thing, she's still a child.'

The women comment freely.

But these surmises are not the reasons for Lily's tears.

The women have so many other things to gossip about—Lily's jewels, her new slippers, her sister's deplorable plight and a lot more.

Lily keeps crying.

Her mother runs up and down frantically, attending to so many things. As for Lizzy's mother, she sits motionless, blinking hard, beside her daughter in a dark recess of the kitchen.

The house rings with excitement.

The honking of a car is heard… The groom's family has arrived. The pandal reverberates with prayer accompanied by music. The groom's sister enters the house bearing a casket holding the bride's new clothes. Another car honks. The kinfolk from Thiruvananthapuram arrive, their silk clothes rustling. Mary comes with Elina. An invitation had been sent to Mary's family too.

It is time to take the bride to the church. They dress her up in that dark room with gold jewels, flowers and a sandal-coloured sari laced with silver zari. A wreath of flowers crowns her forehead. A finely woven diaphanous veil cascades down her back. Her face is not covered though. It is a great disappointment for the village women. But what to do, one has to heed the wishes of the groom's family. Moreover, Mary and Elina had sided with the groom's family in this regard. It is then futile to protest, isn't it?

There is a big commotion outside.

'Bring the bride, hurry, it's time! Be done with your make up.'

Lily falls at her father's feet and seeks his blessings. Tears well up in her eyes. She falls at her mother's feet too. Her mother lifts her up and kisses her cheeks, tears streaming down her eyes. Then...

'Where's the bride going?'

'Where's she going?'

'Kutty, don't you have any sense?'

'Pilley, where are you going?'

Several voices cry out at once. Lily walks straight into the kitchen, her silk sari rustling, saying nothing in reply.

'Akka!'

A figure stands up silently in the darkness.

'Akka! Bless me Akka!' Lizzy breaks into a flood of tears, tears she has been repressing all along. She hugs that tender figure and rains kisses on her cheeks even as her lips tremble.

Lily cries inconsolably. The crowd stands motionless. Their eyes grow moist too. 'What is the Kutty doing there?' Kannapachi's voice rings aloud. Only then are they able to part the sisters.

11

Crime and Punishment

The ruthlessness of summer is truly beyond words, but the skies proclaim that it is finally about to end. For some days now the skies have been overcast. Everyone is drenched in a river of sweat. Every now and then, there is a deep rumble in the west. Lightning flashes incessantly across the sky.

In the midst of all this, the marriage house, that is, Putham Veedu, is wrapped in a funereal silence and wears a deserted look. The pandal has been taken apart. Outside the adichukootu, the ground is strewn with plaited palm leaves and stumps of wooden pegs.

Palmyra climbing proceeds with the usual gusto, though even that will come to a complete standstill once the rains begin. At this moment, when the whole world longs for rain, when the plough and the oxen lie still, only the panaiyeri dreads it. The toddy palms need rain too. Only if it rains well this year, will there be any spathes in the palms the coming year. Still if it rains today, the akkani will be unfit for making jaggery tomorrow.

It must be around four in the morning. The cows bellow loudly, their udders full. It's long since the first cock crowed. Here and there, one hears the noises of birds stirring. Only the crows are still asleep. Not until five do they wake up from their deep Kumbakarnan-like slumber. The *mullai* creeper in the courtyard spreads its gentle fragrance. Lightning cuts across the sky followed by a loud rumble in the west. The noisy rustle of the fronds teased by the winds rises from the palmyras. Through that, one also hears the charak charak sounds of the panaiyeris shinning up and down the palmyras and the kiduk kiduk clatter of their pitchers as they hurry about. Let tomorrow take care of itself. Today, before the rains, one must climb as many trees as one can.

Lightning hisses across the sky.

'Koo...ooo...koo...ooo...' This from a palm near Putham Veedu. Is it Anbaiyan's voice? Why does it sound so strange?

'Koo..Kooo...' A chorus of replies.

'Koo... we're ruined, le! Koo... we're ruined...!'

'What is it, brother?'

'What is it Anbaiyov...?'

'Ayyo, we're ruined!' Anbaiyan is simply unable to say anything else. 'Hurry all of you! Come here at once, le!'

'What is it brother! Has a *mookan* snake bitten you or what?'

Crime and Punishment

'What is it? Tell us!'
'We are almost there, hang on!'
'Why don't you tell us what it is, oi!'
'Has he gone off his head?'
'Get down! Let's go!' They chorus.

But Anbaiyan breaks into a loud wail again, 'Ayyo, we're ruined!' His cry emerges from the pit of his stomach. Thoroughly petrified, he somehow clings to the palm like a lizard on a wall. His hands and legs seem to be functioning on their own.

Lightning streaks across the sky every now and then.

Charak charak. Hurried noises from the palmyras. Then thada thada...the heavy rush of footsteps along with the quick kiduk kiduk rattle of the pitchers.

The panaiyeris come running.

'Amma! We're ruined!' they shriek. Lightning flashes across the sky.

Kannapachi staggers up to the door.

He is about to fall when two people rush to support him. They make him sit and fan his face.

Two women—the daughters-in-law of the house—open the main door and come out to see what the matter is. They run in screaming and wailing.

Lizzy comes out. She raises her hands over her head and runs back screaming, 'Amma!'

The lighting flashes incessantly.

The Upadesi arrives. He reassures Anbaiyan and persuades him to climb down the tree.

Though it is dawn, the skies hang dark and overcast. There is no other light except the frequent flashes of lightning.

The policemen arrive. A narrow *thinnai* runs around Putham Veedu. It is not wide enough for even one person to sit on. It is possible, though, to stretch oneself across its length. There, on a portion of the thinnai that juts out of the adichukootu, lies a body wrapped in a palm mat. It is a human body, all right. But the head is severed.

The head lies on the ground. It is soaked in blood and grime.

The courtyard is packed with people. There are people all over the house. Anbaiyan's wife is trying to revive the women of the house with the help of a few other village women.

'Whose body is this?' asks the inspector.

Whom did he ask?

The Vaidyar arrives. He comes, blinking and perspiring. The news had reached him. Such news spreads like wildfire, doesn't it? He comes alone. Very thoughtful of him, indeed.

'Whose body is this?' the inspector addresses him.

Lightning again.

'My father-in-law's.'

The moustache is clearly visible on the severed head. It is thickly matted with blood, the hair plastered together.

The inspector bends down and picks up a weapon from the ground. It is a knife usually carried by the panaiyeris for cutting palm spathes. It is black with bloodstains. The inspector turns it this way and that.

'Whose knife is this?'

Anbaiyan faints.

'Is this his?'

They check him. There is a similar one on his waist too.

'How did this come here!' Thangaraj, who comes there just then, blurts out.

'Why? Is this yours?'

'Yes, sir. But...'

'Arrest him.'

'Sir, sir...'

Chellappan emerges from the crowd.

'Sir, please give me a moment. Please listen to me, sir.'

'Tell me.'

'It has been nearly four or five days since Annan's knife went missing. It was with this that I chopped vegetables the other day for the marriage feast. It disappeared that very same day. It was here, in this house, that I lost it. This is unjust sir, unjust! Terrible!' There are tears in his eyes.

'It is terrible indeed,' the inspector says curtly, pointing at the severed head lying on the ground. Then he turns to Thangaraj, 'Is there any enmity between you two, oi?' His voice rings with indignation.

Thangaraj swallows hard, 'Enmity? Nothing of that kind, sir!'

A man accompanying the inspector stands taking notes.

Lightning continues to flash across the sky.

The news somehow reaches the women folk inside the house. Anbaiyan's wife and mother come running, pushing their way through the crowd, wailing.

'Amma, has your grandson ever picked a quarrel with this man who lies dead here?' The inspector asks the old woman, Anbaiyan's mother.

'Son, it wasn't you. It was this cursed fellow lying here who threatened you saying he'd cut your head off and all sorts of vile things,' she tells Thangaraj. Then looking at the inspector she says, 'Sir, poor boy, he knows nothing. An innocent child, how will he ever...'

'Is that so?' The inspector turns quickly. 'Arrest him,' he commands.

Thangaraj is handcuffed.

Loud screams, wails, commotion. Even Chellappan sobs inconsolably like a woman, 'Ei Annov! Alas! These cursed fellows have ruined us!'

The inspector goes in to interrogate the women. The dead man's wife lies unconscious. He speaks to her co-sister.

'Where's your husband?'

'I don't know.'

'Has he run away after murdering his brother?'

'Ayyaiyo! He hardly comes home these days. You'll find him either in the toddy shop or the coffee stall.'

'Is it true?' He asks the others.

'Yes,' they acknowledge.

'Was there any animosity between your husband and his brother?'

'Ayyaiyo! He even chopped vegetables for his niece's wedding. How can you even think of it? It's sinful to say such a thing.'

Crime and Punishment

'Amma, I'm merely doing my duty. The truth will emerge in the court. Your husband may be innocent as you say. You needn't fear.'

The day broke over Putham Veedu with this hope.

In a little while, Bhagyam fetched water from the village well. She walked in pertly, bearing news. It was rumoured in the village that the police had taken away Lizzy's father too.

No one kindled the oven fire at Putham Veedu that day.

Lizzy heaped a plate with some leftover rice and fish from a clay pot and took it to Kannapachi. As he quietly refused it, she threw it to the chickens that were scratching around a dirt heap, and gave him a glass of buttermilk instead. He drank it in one gulp, tears streaming down his cheeks. After that, Lizzy had no other work there, so she went in and sat on the steps of the backyard door.

Her eyes wandered in the direction of Anbaiyan's house and stayed riveted there.

No smoke curled out of their chimney either.

There, in the courtyard of their house, a few chickens ran around the haystack, pecking at something and chasing one another.

In a way, the sight of them assuaged her grief.

How gutsy and beautiful the country rooster looked! How soft its wings were, how colourful and resplendent! Only the peacock's feather could surpass it. Yes, the peacock's feather.

And so many little chicks. Their wings had not fully-grown yet. Lizzy counted them. The mind had to be kept occupied. Otherwise how it wandered!

Mother hen, mother hen, come hatch your eggs!
Wander the yard, your chicks trailing after your legs!

What was that song? She had often sung it while carrying little Lily on her hip. Now Lily was no longer a child. And there was no one to sing the song either.

Songs! What of them now? Didn't one hear songs all the time in the neighbouring house? But all that was in the past. Chellappan—the precious child of that family—what work did he have except learning some film song or the other and humming it to his heart's content? What happened to those songs now? Why had everything fallen silent? Why? Why?

Her head reeled. How was it that her heart kept wandering over to Thangaraj's house despite all that had happened.

Would they beat a person black and blue in the lock-up?

Who would they beat? Thangaraj? Appan?

But who had done it?

What did it matter? They would beat her Appan. Her whole body ached. All said and done, he was her Appan, her own flesh and blood. What did it matter whether they beat her Appan or her? Wasn't it all the same?

She had seen policemen when she was a little child. She used to wander freely on the roads back then. Policemen! They aroused fear, a feeling of terror.

Yes, the policemen had taken them away. Who? Appan, Thangaraj.

How the heart kept going around in circles!

They had taken Thangaraj away but how did it matter to her?

Who was he to her?

Would they be tied up and beaten? She had heard that they would make a man confess to crimes he hadn't even committed.

Did Thangaraj do it? Who had done it then?

How does a headless body look? How had it looked?

Whose body did they say it was? Was it really Chithappa's body that lay severed in two?

Why did the blood appear black? Thick black lumps all over the ground.

It seemed Lily couldn't even get up from her bed, Bhagyam told them. Lily didn't even get to see her father's body. The policemen had carried it away.

Police, red caps.

How did Lily feel now?

Mother hen, mother hen, come hatch your eggs!

Wander the yard, your chicks trailing after your legs!

Such a joyful song. It felt so good to look at those little chicks!

Was she going mad?

That should never happen. Come what may, she should never lose her head.

What a coward she was!

Her mother clearly had more grit than her. Ammai had had to confront so much in her life. So many failures! Still, had she ever thrown herself into a pit or a pond? Why should Lizzy alone... Was it enough if one was educated? Whatever happens, she must face it courageously. After all, that was life, wasn't it?

What more could happen? Could it be worse than what had already passed?

She must stop this turmoil in her mind or else she'd go raving mad.

Her Ammai had no one else. Nor did her Kannapachi.

Madness? Was it new to her? Hadn't she turned insane a long time ago? That day, when Thangaraj had looked at her face and said, 'I wish to ask your father for your hand. Do I have your consent?'—her madness had begun that very same day.

Why did she keep picturing his face all the time?

It seemed the knife was his. Did he do it then? What if they found some evidence? Weren't people hanged for such a crime?

What about her Appan?

Why did her body and spirit cringe at the thought of him?

She must think of that hen and its chicks. Such lovely little ones. Like children. Like goat kids. Like kittens. Why couldn't she have stayed a child forever?

Were she a child, she could have played on her father's lap and smiled at her mother even if her mother wept.

She didn't realize that tears were blinding her eyes.

Suddenly, she heard her father's voice behind her. It sounded real. No! It was not an illusion.

'Kutty, Lizzy!'

'Appa!'

She rushed to hug his feet but withdrew seeing the steely look in his eyes.

Her mother stood before him, crying.

'If there's some leftover kanji bring me some, I'm hungry.' There was no tenderness in his voice.

Lizzy hurriedly brought him some leftover kanji. He gulped it down quickly.

'Is there more? I'm hungry.'

She brought some more. He ate.

It gave her anguished heart some solace. Suddenly, she felt hungry too. Ravenous like an elephant.

'Kannapachi! Will you drink some kanji?'

'No, Kutty.'

The mother and daughter sat facing each other as they ate. Chithi was no longer at home. Her brother had forcefully taken her away in a taxi. Her son-in-law had called her to his house too but how could she go to her daughter's house for the first time in such a state?

'Ei, old hag! Guess who bailed me out?'

Terrified, Lizzy's mother looked at her husband.

'Ei, it was your son-in-law. Why do you look at me that way? The Vaidyan is so full of concern for this father-in-law. Do you know that, hag?'

Lizzy felt her stomach turn.

'Listen, you hag! Have you gone dumb? You look as if you've lost your husband. Haven't I returned, hale and hearty?'

'Don't you know what to speak? Should I go through that horror too?' Ammai started crying in a loud voice.

'*Ada*, ugly crone! Stop wailing. The house has prospered well, thanks to your constant wailing!'

Lizzy's mother stopped crying. Lizzy felt angry and pained. Who was responsible for the wonderful plight of her family? Her Appan or her Ammai? Her father continued, 'He'll learn his lessons now. I've returned after enrolling him in that school, so he'll learn his lessons well. How is that, old crone? Isn't that nice?'

'What are you saying?'

He pointed to the house behind theirs. Lizzy understood. Thangaraj was languishing in some lock-up or jail. He hadn't been granted bail.

The drunkard pulled out a mat, stretched himself on it and started snoring. His wife sat beside him and sighed deeply.

How was he able to sleep so soundly? He was fortunate indeed.

Lizzy went back to sit on the steps of the backyard door. She sat there for a long time.

Was that Chellappan coming towards her? She could hardly recognize him. His eyes were red, as if blood had congealed in them. His face was drawn, his cheeks wan.

'Akka!'

This was the first time Chellappan had addressed her thus. He had spoken to her once or twice before but only when it had been absolutely necessary. Though seventeen years of age, he was still a small boy in her eyes. Nevertheless, she avoided speaking to him. Why invite unnecessary trouble?

'What is it, Chellappa?' The same thought arose in their hearts, the same figure. Their eyes filled with tears.

'Annan sent word...' He began to sob and couldn't speak.

'Tell me, Chellappa.' She was anxious to know.

'Anna said...whatever...whatever...happens... Whatever happens to him, you...' Loud sobs.

'I...I...' Lizzy fumbled.

'You...must believe... Just that is enough... You must forget everything else... We may not be able to see Annan again...' The young man again broke into a flood of tears.

Lizzy didn't notice him weeping for she was herself weeping inconsolably, covering her face with her hands. With great difficulty she pulled herself together and asked, 'What should I believe, Chellappa?'

'Annan didn't do it. I swear he didn't do it. He's not capable of hurting even a worm.' Chellappan regained his composure.

'I believe it, Chellappa. I believe every word of it. You go tell him that.'

'I will.'

'Also tell him this. He must never ask me to forget him. Tell him I can't forget him. Once, at school, I got the teacher to cane him, now I've got him the gallows. Is there any justice in asking me to forget that, Chellappa? Tell me, you tell me?'

They cried quietly.

'Appa has returned.'

'I know.'

'He's sleeping.'

'...'

'You tell him this too. A worthy man must not think of a murderer's daughter—that's not right. What's written on her forehead is something else. Doesn't the daughter have a part in her father's crime? Ask him to forget me Chellappa.'

'....'

'I am the cause of all these troubles. But he must not blame me. Ask him to regard it as fate's cruel play, thambi!'

'....'

She cried.

He cried.

'Akka, if there's a God...'

'Is there a God, thambi? You go, Appan may wake up.'

'If there's a God won't he unite the two of you?'

'What do I know? I'm just a bit of chaff tossed by the winds. Please get going, Chellappa. Appan may wake up.'

'My Appan will kill me too.'

'Don't say that word again, Chellappa!'

'No, Akka, I won't.' He left. She entered the house too, wiping her face with the end of her sari.

It was her father who greeted her. His face was distorted with rage.

'Who was it, Kutty?'

'....'

'You daughter of a slut! I said, who was it?'

'....'

He stepped forward, and raised his hand. Had Lizzy looked scared or even flinched, that blow would have surely fallen on her. But he was taken aback by the way she stood there. She stood staring at him, an immovable stone. The flood had risen well over the dam. What was the point in being scared?

Terrified, her mother came running.

'Why are you killing her?'

'Isn't she your beloved daughter? I knew you would ask, knew you would certainly ask. Which illicit suitor did you let her talk to, eh?'

'Look at the state she's in and watch what you say. Why don't you just push her into some pit or pond, instead?'

How contrary this was to the usual state of affairs! Her father was about to thrash her and her mother had run to her rescue. Strange world!

'You hag! I'm not lying. I saw that fellow leave. You ask her if you wish. Ask your daughter yourself. Then tell me what to do. I'll do as you bid. The culprit! Look how she stands! She has begun her tricks, hasn't she? Pretentious whore!'

He ground his teeth. His wife stood by uncertainly.

Someone gently pushed open the main door. It was the new son-in-law of the family. How many terrible things had come about ever since he set foot in the family. He came in, hanging his head as if he were the criminal. He looked worn out.

The small group broke up. Lizzy sought refuge in the darkness of the kitchen. Her mother followed her.

'Sit down, son,' said Lizzy's father.

The Vaidyar sat on a reed mat.

'You must all come and stay in my house for a few days. Lily has sent word.'

'Will it look nice, son?' A sheepish grin. 'We are more than grateful for the help you have rendered now.'

The Vaidyar looked a little relieved. 'I think the case will turn out in our favour.'

'Mm...'

'Our lawyer said so. He said he wouldn't rest till he sends that fellow to the gallows. Lily is anxious that he shouldn't get away with it. She has been crying day and night.'

'Mm...come, Appan is in the adichukootu.'

Lizzy couldn't hear the rest of the conversation. Only noise filled her ears, a meaningless rush of noise. The conversation continued in the adichukootu. Wasn't that Kannapachi's voice? What did it matter to her?

Lizzy's father came in after sending away the Vaidyar. His steps faltered. He looked very tired. His voice sounded weary too.

'Ei, old hag, where's that Kutty?'

'Here. I am here, Appa!' What did Lizzy have to fear now? Whom did she have to fear?

'Kutty! Jump into some pit or pond and get lost. I said get lost! That's the only thing that hasn't happened so far,' he roared.

There was no defiance in her voice, only dissent.

'Appa, why should I kill myself? Our family fell into ruin a long time ago. I didn't die then and neither did I bring dishonour to my Appan. Am I going to die now because

some other family is about to be ruined?'
Her mother was puzzled. But every word she spoke hit her father hard. His eyes grew red. He trembled.
'Appa, you needn't fear. I'll never bring disgrace to you. Here, like her, I know how to keep my body and soul together,' Lizzy pointed at her mother.
His face fell.
Just then Kannapachi called from the adichukootu, 'Lizzyamma?' Lizzy hurried to him.
'Be here, my child. Is it true then, what I heard?'
'What did you hear, Kannapachi?'
'It seems that fellow came to speak to you, on the pretext of giving keerai seeds?'
'Yes.'
'I believe he came again and again, the cursed fellow?'
'...'
'Why didn't you tell us?'
'I was scared something terrible might happen.'
'It has happened now, hasn't it? He asked for our girl and not stopping at that...'
He couldn't continue. His voice faltered.
'How did you come to know all this, Kannapachi?'
'The Vaidyar told me. Your sister Lily has been crying to him. When they hang the fellow, I'll go, even if I have to totter all the way with my stick.'
There was such spite in Kannapachi's words, his face and his ageing eyes. That same old spite!
Lizzy quietly went back inside.

Everyone believed that Thangaraj was the murderer. Everyone, but her Appan and herself. When all was said and done, only she had the ability to understand her father in that house.

He was lying stretched on a mat. Perhaps he didn't wish to see her face. His eyes were closed.

Appan had murdered her Chithappa. It caused her such anguish to think of it. But that murder had been committed for her! So she had a part in it now. Thangaraj would be hanged. That would be murder too! That murder would also be for her. Alas, was she born a girl just for this?

They say it is the woman who begets and the woman who destroys. In her case, though, she seemed to be leaving behind only a trail of destruction.

They were trying to foist her father's crime on Thangaraj. What could she do? Even if she were to tell anyone what she knew, what good would it do? It wouldn't help Thangaraj at all. Besides, it would be a blow to everyone in her family including her Kannapachi. They would somehow save the criminal and send Thangaraj to the gallows with the lawyer's help. Who could then bear what would ensue? There would be trouble after trouble.

That night Lizzy didn't sleep.

Perhaps because he had slept during the day, her father tossed and turned and kept moaning in his sleep. It was the wee hours of morning and Lizzy was just about to drift into sleep when she woke up, startled, on hearing a faint moan, 'Lizzyamma!' She ran to her father. His face was distorted.

Crime and Punishment

When he attempted to speak, a reddish froth foamed at his mouth.

'Amma! Amma!' Lizzy screamed. 'Amma, ask Bhagyam to fetch the Vaidyar,' she cried out to her mother while supporting her father's head in her hands.

His condition worsened before the Vaidyar could come. He drifted into unconsciousness. He grew delirious and talked wildly. They only understood bit and parts of what he said.

'Kutty! Look, I murdered him. What does it matter to you?'

'What are you saying?' cried his wife.

He glared at her. 'Ei, Hag! What do you know? One swift stroke and it fell in two,' he jeered.

Kannapachi came there tapping his stick but went back to the adichukootu, not comprehending what was going on.

'Chopped vegetables, did I? I chopped his head off. You can't imagine how well that knife cuts!'

'Ayyaiyo! What is he raving?' lamented his wife.

Lizzy didn't open her mouth.

The Vaidyar arrived. Lizzy rose to leave. Her mother didn't move. Was this the time to observe formalities?

Appan seemed to recognize the Vaidyar.

'Here he comes. He who led us on and ruined us! Didn't you lead my daughter on? That panaiyeri fellow...he laid a trap for her! I came to know about it!'

The Vaidyar bent down to feel the pulse.

'His own child meant so much to my brother. My brother

called my child "Pilley, Pilley" as if she were his own daughter and my child, poor thing, stood wide-eyed. But he saw to it that his own daughter got married. Ei panaiyeri, *my* daughter doesn't need you. Never ever will she accept you!'

'Mama, you must lie still. Try and get some sleep.'

'Ei, I'm going to sleep. Sleep soundly. I won't get up even if you try to wake me up. Call my child. Lizzyamma! Where did you go? Ei, I said call my child.'

The Vaidyar didn't know what to do. He blinked. But the sick man's wife called in a tearful voice, 'Lizzyamma, come see your Appan. O, I simply can't bear to see it all.' She wailed loudly.

Lizzy came back into the room.

She didn't feel embarrassed that the Vaidyar was standing there too and didn't take any notice of him. She sat near her father and took his hand in hers.

'Have you come, my child? Daughter, it is true that you are a murderer's daughter, but you are good.'

'Appa, don't speak, Appa!'

'Let me talk now, my daughter! Look here, you'll live well. You are my daughter. But... I have sent that fellow to the gallows. You needn't fear anything now. Come here, child,' his tongue faltered as he brought Lizzy's head closer to him.

'I am not blessing you. My hands are tainted. After this drunkard is gone, take your Kannapachi's blessings... There's a suitor coming from Thiruvananthapuram to marry my daughter!' He rambled incoherently.

He frothed at the mouth again. With great difficulty, he

managed to say, 'Ei, Upadesi! Young Upadesi! Have you come to send me to heaven? Even if you send me there, I'll come back to haunt you, you just wait and see.'

He was right. It was indeed the Upadesi. It was surprising that he had managed to recognize him. This new Upadesi had come in the place of the one that Thangaraj had approached. The new Upadesi was a spirited young man, interested in God's work. He was always surrounded by a band of eager young men. One or two accompanied him now.

As soon as they saw the Upadesi, Lizzy and her mother stepped aside half-heartedly. Lizzy noticed the Vaidyar throw up his hands dejectedly on seeing him. Then he went out to the adichukootu. Perhaps he was going to inform Kannapachi. Lizzy lay whimpering on her mother's lap. Could her grief surpass her mother's?

The visitors surrounded the dying man. In spite of her anguish, Lizzy looked up to see if they would utter some prayer or psalm but she only saw them speaking in urgent, hushed tones. Appan made some gestures every now and then. He moved his lips. They watched his lips closely. Suddenly, everything fell silent. No one spoke. Finally, the Upadesi stood up and walked to the adichukootu, slowly, quietly.

Lizzy understood. A loud wail emerged from the pit of her throat. Her mother and Bhagyam joined her.

The Upadesi returned and consoled the women, 'Amma, don't cry. This world is not ours forever.' But would they pay heed, those who sat there wailing?

They fixed the funeral for the same day. They laid the body in a coffin, covered it with heaps of jasmine and roses and closed it. Lizzy showered some flowers on the body too. Lily didn't come. For some reason, the Vaidyar refused to bring her. He stood with the crowd and participated in the rites.

A few young men arrived to carry the coffin. Before they lifted the coffin, the Upadesi began singing a hymn. Those men and women who were in a position to sing, joined him. Many couldn't control their tears as they sang. Their voices trembled. Lizzy was in no position to sing. Nevertheless, the song filled her ears.

After the hymn was sung, the Bible was read. It was the chapter usually read at funerals. It had been read out during Kannammai's funeral too. But never had those lines touched her heart as deeply as they did now.

'For all flesh is as grass, and all glory of man as the flower of grass. The grass withereth and the flower thereof fadeth away.'

'The grass withereth and the flower thereof fadeth away...'

Yes, who had engraved those lines in her heart? They seemed so familiar! Lizzy did not register the prayers being said. She could only cry. Even Kannapachi was weeping like a child.

The coffin was lifted. Lizzy tried to console her mother, who wailed beating her chest. The Vaidyar stayed behind to support Kannapachi.

In the midst of her anguish, Lizzy had a small consolation.

Crime and Punishment

Her father didn't go to the gallows. He wasn't executed. He was carried away, bedecked with flowers, like a groom. Like all good people. Like her own Kannammai. At least in death he was able to salvage his honour. The family could take pride in that.

Lizzy remained dazed for two days and then, suddenly, she felt like reading some old books. All the dailies and monthly magazines that Mary Akka had brought for her Chithi years ago, lay scattered in a wooden chest. Plump house crickets, brown as dates, jumped out as she rifled through the chest. Some fell on her face and head. She could at least pass some time rummaging the contents of that old chest. When she took out the books one by one, a child's school reader fell open. There was a peacock's feather between its pages. Just the eye. It was certainly not the one she had given to Thangaraj. It must have belonged to Lily. Lizzy sat there for a long time staring at that feather.

There was no one to remind her that she should arrange the scattered books back in the trunk.

Suddenly, the peacock feather appeared to grow long. It looped and curled and entwined itself around her feet. She woke up, crying aloud. No, no it was not a snake. She realized that she had fallen asleep from exhaustion.

12

The Verdict

Anbaiyan couldn't believe his ears. His son was going to be released!

The day Lizzy's father was buried, the Upadesiyar had gone to Anbaiyan's house straight from the graveyard. He had sat there talking for a long time. A few important facts, he said, had come to light from the delirious utterances of the deceased man; consequently, he and his friends wished to meet Anbaiyan's lawyer. Utterly devastated and grief stricken by his son's plight, Anbaiyan lay a shattered man, confined to his bed, unable to even move. His hair had turned completely grey within a few days and he looked haggard and old. On hearing the Upadesi's reassuring words, he sat up eagerly. When hope springs in the heart, one's hands and legs automatically regain strength. Anbaiyan got ready to accompany them. When they were about to leave, his mother came there weeping and wailing.

'Son, I heard it all with my own ears. That cursed fellow who perished the other day, it was he who came and threatened my grandson. "I'll cut your head off, see if I don't," he said. Now you tell me son, only they are capable of such things. Will we ever dream of doing something like that? I told the inspector the other day, son. I swear on you, I told him. Did he listen to this old woman? Who will listen to this old woman? Tell me, son!' She complained bitterly to the Upadesiyar, tears streaming down her cheeks.

'Amma, what did you tell the inspector?'

'I told you just now! Didn't that fellow say he would cut my grandson's head off? I told him about that.'

The Upadesiyar glanced meaningfully at his friends who had accompanied him. They smiled.

'Amma, you needn't interfere in this. Isn't it enough if your grandson returns home safely?' consoled the Upadesiyar.

But her daughter-in-law was thoroughly agitated, 'Enough! Enough! I'll live to see that. Will they live well, those fellows who accused my son?' she wept.

'Don't say that Amma! Why carry such bitterness in your heart? Leave it in God's hands.'

But she was only vexed by what he said. 'What do you know Ayya? Only a mother can understand it all, what do you know?' she burst out, not letting go.

The Upadesiyar could only hang his head before her sorrow. 'True!' he acknowledged.

The menfolk prepared to leave. When they set out,

Anbaiyan was seized by a fond hope. However, it didn't appear that the case would be resolved all that easily. Lily's Mama from Thiruvananthapuram sat next to the prosecutor, with fierce determination. Lily's husband was ready to spend any amount of money just to assuage her tears. For some days, he even forgot his patients. Anbaiyan's lawyer lacked expertise. Besides, Anbaiyan didn't possess much cash in hand. Every bit of their earnings had been invested in land. Now, all of a sudden, when they wanted to sell everything, who would want to buy it? Also, what could be done when people desired to make the most of the situation? Even if someone did come forward to buy, who was there to go out and make enquiries? Anbaiyan had turned very old all of a sudden. Relentless crying had reduced Chellappan, that 17-year-old young man, to a helpless child. Only their distant relative, Thangaiyan, the old panaiyeri of Putham Veedu, kept visiting them, rendering whatever help he could. But Anbaiyan wished he would stop coming. Thangaiyan was an 'Old Testament man.' An eye for an eye. A tooth for a tooth. The rich persecute the poor so the poor must hit back at the rich. Such was his philosophy. Anbaiyan was anxious not to beget fresh trouble. Thus any association with Thangaiyan didn't seem desirable.

The land could not be sold.

The trial seemed to be heading neither here nor there.

Despite the Upadesiyar's reassurances, Anbaiyan was more frightened than hopeful.

But then, good news finally arrived. Thangaraj was finally

going to come home tomorrow!'

'Let him first come. One mustn't believe everything. What if one's hopes are shattered? What if...'

It was Anbaiyan and the Upadesiyar who brought Thangaraj home. Everyone in his family wholeheartedly blessed the Upadesiyar for the efforts he had taken to save Thangaraj.

But grief, anger and bitterness far outweighed the joy of having their son home again. The mother caught hold of both his hands and wept inconsolably. She suffered to see him so utterly changed, a shadow of his former self. The grandmother didn't tire of cursing those at Putham Veedu. Even Anbaiyan carped at the behaviour of the so-called respectable folk with a rancour that was very unlike him. Thangaiyan spurred him on. Only Chellappan tried to talk light-heartedly.

Thangaraj kept quiet through all this talk and tears. His expression was grim.

The Upadesiyar hardly spoke. He was struck speechless by their excitement and agitation.

News of the Upadesiyar's efforts had reached Lizzy's ears too. On the whole, her family was very unhappy with him. They felt that he was acting against them. Not that the panaiyeris approved of him. They had their misgivings too. It was a common opinion among them that he did all this merely to earn a good name. Whether or not he desired a good name, the Upadesiyar felt thoroughly satisfied—you could even say proud—as if he had accomplished a difficult feat. After all, he was a human being too!

When Lizzy learned that Thangaraj might be acquitted of the crime, she was filled with a new hope. There was no one to reproach her now, at least not as before. Her Appan and Chithappan were no more. As for her Ammai, she was certain that she could somehow convince her; if not now, at least in the future. But she soon realized she was wrong. On the day Thangaraj returned, film music blared from his house, thanks to Chellappan. Kannapachi and Ammai sat with grim, expressionless faces. The rift between the two families had only deepened further. Earlier it was just a matter of the respectable and the inferior. But now they were enemies too. Earlier she had to challenge everyone's stubborn will and family pride, whereas now she would be shattering love and hope. Kannapachi and Ammai looked to her. The love and trust they placed on her kept them alive. Wasn't she their only succour now? Should she crush the two, who now seemed like helpless children, trample on their trust and mercilessly abandon them in her pursuit of a happy life with Thangaraj?

Theivame, theivame, theivame!

What sort of a secure, happy life was she striving after?

Could a girl hope to do anything in her life without her family's support?

It was impossible for her to betray her Kannapachi and Ammai. Even though her heart was hardened, it hadn't turned to a pitiless stone.

And yet...

She felt she would go mad at the very thought of

Thangaraj. Were he to meet her just one more time and tell her, 'Lizzy! I have forgiven your father. You must consent to be my wife,' would her legs automatically follow him?

Be quiet you foolish heart!

He had laid siege to her thoughts! Was it his handsome face, his youth or his smile?

Perhaps these were the reasons. Nevertheless, weren't circumstances to be blamed too?

It seemed that Lily's husband was desperately hunting for a groom for her. Who wanted his kindness? How could she consent to marriage if he turned up with a suitor one fine day? Wouldn't that amount to deceiving someone? Should she be guilty of that too? In any case, she knew a way out of that.

She was racked by the thought that Thangaraj still hadn't come to see her. Would he come? Or would he stay away?

He came. But this time he didn't approach her with fear and hesitation. He came the day after he returned from prison. After a long, inner struggle, he had reached a decision.

It was around the time she usually sat near the backyard door watching the chicken.

'Lizzy...!'

Never before had she heard him utter her name. But it didn't sound strange to her ears. She felt as if she had been hearing it all her life.

She didn't run away this time. Was she the old Lizzy? Wasn't she now a murderer's daughter? As for him, hadn't he just returned after staring death in the face? Whom should they fear? She descended the steps quietly and stood facing him, expecting to hear more from him.

But she couldn't control her tears. She couldn't even bring herself to look at his face.

'Lizzy!'

No reply. Only tears.

'Are you happy that I have come back, Lizzy? Were you scared that I may not return?'

'Happiness, sorrow, from now on, how does it all matter to me?'

'It seems you told my brother that you'll never forget how the teacher caned me or that you sent me to the gallows, is that true?'

'...'

'If you care so much for me, come with me now. This instant.'

'No!'

'Why not? What else can be done? Do you still dream that your family will send you to me with pomp and splendour?'

'...'

'That will never happen, Lizzy, never. How else do you think I can marry you?'

'...'

'Then why do you drive me mad?'

'What did I do? I also told your brother something else. Have you forgotten that?'

'What did you tell him?'

The Verdict

'That you must forget me. It all happened because of me. You must forget and forgive me. Didn't I tell you this?' Again a flood of tears.

He stood silent for a while, looking at her face.

'What's the use of crying?' he asked angrily.

'I simply don't know what to do. How can I go with you? How can you ask me to do that?'

'What else can I do, tell me?'

'I told you, forget me. I can see no other way.'

'Lizzy! Do you ask me to forget you? If it were so easy, I would have done that by now. Look here, you know that it's not possible. I know that too.'

She looked at his face with pity.

'How can I go with you? Kannapachi and Ammai will die if I do that. Are you saying that we can live happily, peacefully after that?'

'You needn't come. And none will see me in this village hereafter or even utter my name.'

'No!'

'All a girl ever does is cry. Lizzy, will you come with me or not?' His voice was tinged with sadness, anticipation and urgency.

'What will your family say?'

'Nothing. If they do, I'll go back to the gallows.'

'They will never say a harsh word to you. But, what about me?'

'....'

'See, didn't I tell you?'

'Lizzy! Why should you care about all that? It's my love for you that matters, isn't it?'

'Yes, I need only your love. But one thing... it's enough if my own conscience doesn't prick me. Otherwise... I can't bear to think of it.'

'You and your conscience. I'll go away. Then don't search for me.'

He turned to leave.

'Please wait.'

He turned back angrily. But one look at her eyes and he softened.

'Please listen to me. Just give me two days. I can't do much. I'll try my best. Then I'll send word. Ask Chellappan to meet me.'

'What if you can do nothing?'

'Let's face it then. All said and done, I am my father's girl. I'm not scared of being flogged or thrashed.'

A mischievous smile appeared on his face.

'There's nobody to flog you now.'

'Yes...' she wept.

'Then what are you frightened of?'

'Look, if I go with you, you must trust me. You must have trust in my love for you.'

'Lizzy!'

'Then I mustn't let down trust and affection. If I do that, love will eventually forsake me. I can't betray Kannapachi and Ammai.'

'There... Your mother!'

The Verdict

'Let her be, let her see us, she must know someday!'

'Lizzy Kutty! Kutty, Lizzy!' her mother screamed from the house. 'Wretch! What are you doing there?'

'In a way, it's good,' muttered Lizzy. 'I am coming Amma!' she shouted in reply but didn't budge from her place.

Her mother had to come out. She raised her hands over her head and started wailing loudly.

Thangaraj stood stunned.

Lizzy approached her mother and said, 'Amma! Bless us!'

Thangaraj beamed with pride.

The old woman rushed in, beating her chest, lamenting. While Lizzy followed her, Thangaraj remained standing outside.

The matter reached the adichukootu. Lizzy's mother stood behind the one of the doors, protesting and wailing in a loud tone to her father-in-law. This wasn't the time to observe formalities, was it?

Kannapachi called Lizzy. This was the most testing moment of her life.

'Theivame, theivame, theivame,' she prayed fervently.

She went and stood behind the other door. What to do! She couldn't bear to see Kannapachi face to face. She had to hide herself even from him.

The accused stood on one side and the accuser on the other.

'Lizzyamma!'

'Kannapachi!'

'What is Ammai saying?'

'Ask her!' shouted her mother vehemently.

'It's true, Kannapachi!'

'The father hardly bothered that there was a grown up girl at home and her father's father doesn't care either. Some sly fox is going to carry away all the property and a worthless panaiyeri is going to walk away with the girl. Let father-in-law guard the property; let him cry over it; who cares if some cur or spirit whisks the girl away.' Her mother burned with rage.

Sweat ran down the old man's face and bare chest. He flung his towel over his shoulder. He reached for his stick. He also picked up his palm visiri out of habit. The loose folds of skin on his large, wrinkled arms shook as he made an effort to stand up. He set out with great difficulty, carrying his huge paunch before him.

'Where are you going now?' Lizzy's mother asked him.

'To Lily's house. Must see the Vaidyar.' After all, there was no other male member from whom they could seek help.

'You might faint in this blazing sun, Kannapachi.'

When he reached the gate he turned back. There was a vacant look in his eyes.

'Do you really care about this old man?' Those words wrenched Lizzy's heart. How utterly disillusioned he sounded!

The mother and daughter sat opposite each other in the ill-lit kitchen. They didn't speak. How convenient it was, that darkness. They needn't see each other's face.

A storm would be raging in the Vaidyar's house now.

Was there really a storm?

The Verdict

The Vaidyar had just returned home, tired after calling on his patients. And right then, Kannapachi walked in.

Lily came out to see him, her eyes swollen and red with weeping.

Lily wasn't received all that happily in the family. The endless concessions her husband gave her was one of the reasons. Her family's disgrace and the hassles with the case was another.

Such was life.

Now another blow!

Was Akka so daring? The cursed wretch! Wasn't she to be blamed for all that had happened? How could Lily even think of her as her 'Akka', henceforth?

In a way, wasn't Lizzy also responsible for her father's death? It was only because she ensnared that fellow, Thangaraj, that enmity had arisen between him and her father. When she had pleaded with her husband about the case, he had raised all sorts of doubts about her Periyappa, poor man! He had even refused to take her to her Periyappa's funeral. Now let him understand, let him judge for himself who was right. It was all Lizzy's fiendish plot. That panaiyeri fellow of hers... Had the court really acquitted him? What sort of justice was this!

Lily's anger and bitterness turned to tears.

Her husband sat listening quietly to what Kannapachi was saying.

'Son, you must find a fellow one way or another so she can be married off as early as possible!'

After much thought, the Vaidyar replied carefully, '*Thatha*, what's the use of marrying her off to someone like that?'

'Listen to that, Kannapachi! He seems to have no thought for the family's respectability!' Lily wept in grief.

'It is not that, Thatha! Previously, despite my mother's protests I spent my money on the court case, as I couldn't bear to see Lily's tears. But I made a mistake, Thatha. I had my suspicions even then. Only now everything is clear. By God's grace justice has finally been done. Thangaraj didn't commit the murder. Certainly not! Ask the Upadesiyar if you wish.'

'Ayyo!' cried Lily.

'There's no need to go the Upadesi, son. All that is over and done with. What I ask you now is a different matter altogether. Son, do you ask me to give our girl to a panaiyeri?'

'Thatha! Times have changed. If that is your objection you have already given one of your girls into a panaiyeri's family, haven't you?'

'What?'

'Yes. My grandfather's father was a panaiyeri. So can it be said, once a panaiyeri always a panaiyeri?'

Lily blinked.

'Oh that's right, Annan has seen it all, hasn't he? Why, wasn't he the one who raised his great-grandfather?' fumed the Vaidyar's sister Kanakam, who had been standing there quietly for sometime.

'Bundle up your empty pride, Kutty. I merely stated the facts, Thatha. Whether you like it or not, this is the situation

The Verdict

in your family. How can we now marry her off to someone else? What if she later elopes with him...?'

'Will the husband keep quiet? Won't he kill her?' Lily couldn't take it any longer. Had her marriage taken place according to her wishes? Who had cared for her wish that day? But wasn't she happy now?

'Lily! You're still so immature. What's all this talk of killing and flaying? What can be done after she elopes? Haven't we had enough of killing and murder? Do you want more?'

Lily went in, crying.

'Son, all said and done, how can we give our girl to a fellow who climbs the palms for a livelihood?'

Kannapachi was very weary. His protests were now feeble.

'If that boy really loves your girl, ask him to give up palmyra climbing for the sake of her family. Won't he listen? The tamarind business is much more profitable and he already has some experience in it. You can ask him to do that, can't you?'

Kannapachi sat silent for a long time. The Vaidyar continued, 'What do you say, Thatha? Shall we go ahead and get them married? Poor fellow, let's do him a good turn for all the trouble we gave him. She'll also be happy. What matters more to you, Thatha? The happiness of two goodhearted children or your family pride?'

'Son, these are your times; things are not what they used to be in my day. I don't understand any of this. Do as you please. I am an old man. I have one foot in the grave. My sons, the ones who had to bear my coffin, have departed before me, like Abel and Cain. Must I die destroying the happiness of these tender buds?'

Did Lizzy, who was at Putham Veedu, imagine that it would all materialize so easily?

Her mother first railed against her father-in-law. But now the situation had turned completely in Lizzy's favour. How long could the protest of a single heart last? A tide of emotions swept the entire family in one direction like small twigs being carried away by a flooded river.

◆

Lizzy's wedding. And it was the Vaidyar who made all the arrangements. The Upadesiyar too showed a special interest in the marriage.

Thangaiyan, the old panaiyeri, once again took charge of the palms at Putham Veedu. Kannapachi didn't show any resentment in this matter. His heart overflowed with a new sense of contentment. Hadn't Lizzy promised that she would never ever forsake her Kannapachi?

When Thangaiyan arrived, Lizzy had a wish. Where was Pethi? She had been so eager to come to her marriage!

It was two years since Pethi had been buried. Who would think of her now? *The grass withereth and the flower thereof fadeth away.* Yes, our lives are like the grass and flowers.

Preparations were underway for the marriage. Lizzy stopped showing up at the backyard of their house. She hardly saw Chellapan these days.

The Verdict

Barring the two young men, the others in Anbaiyan's family didn't wholeheartedly approve of the marriage. Nevertheless, they kept quiet. After all, the son had returned from the jaws of death. As long as he was happy what did it matter to them? However, Anbaiyan was unyielding when the issue of palmyra climbing came up.

'Let him listen to his wife's family if he wants to. Why should I? I may be able to climb the palms for another year or perhaps two, who knows? As long as there is strength in my hands and legs I will continue climbing the palms. Do these fellows know the worth of a panaiyeri? A time will come when people will rue the dearth of panaiyeris,' he said to those who had come to congratulate him on the marriage.

In his heart of heart, he took pride in the marriage. Wasn't the bride from a respectable family? Not that he was in any way inferior to them. Hadn't he fathered two fine, sturdy sons? Soon Chellappan would go to college and return a graduate. What more could he want?

After much struggle, Lily's husband pacified her. She reluctantly agreed to go to her house to be of assistance to her *Periammai*. She thought that Kannapachi and Periammai overindulged Lizzy. Where was the need to pamper her thus? Didn't they have any sense? It served them right, whatever had happened! But for the sake of appearances and in order to please her husband she behaved with courtesy. She took part in everything, albeit with some detachment.

No invitation was sent to Mary's house. Lizzy told her mother that it wasn't necessary to invite them.

However, an invitation was posted to their relations in Thiruvananthapuram. But it didn't look like they would come. Wasn't Chithi at Thiruvananthapuram now?

The pandal was erected. There wasn't much of a crowd in the pandal. But people would surely turn up on the day of the marriage. Wasn't it a typical village wedding? Everyone was invited, so they would at least come to partake of the feast.

Dressed beautifully, her hair adorned with flowers, Lizzy walked up and down the house. Her pleasant smile, the old smile that lit up her face, had at last returned. The secret of Lizzy's beauty lay in her heart's happiness. Her face was radiant, so much so that the village women who paid their visit, couldn't help noticing it. They were all praise for her. After all, when would she look beautiful, if not now?

Just two more days remained until the wedding. Lizzy is reading the Bible aloud for Kannapachi. How Kannapachi totters up to the pandal every now and then!

Chellappan walks in.

'Akka! No...no, Anni!'

She looks up. Her face turns crimson. Chellappan's face is shining with mischief and happiness.

'Annan is waiting outside. He wishes to see you.'

'Tell him I can't come.'

'He wants to know what colour sari he must choose for you.'

'Tell him he needn't ask me anything.'

'No, he wants to see you.'

'Tell him I can't see him now.'

Chellappan laughs.

'What's this, Anni? You message for Annan sounds so different now', he teases her.

Her face reddens like a *kovai* fruit. She closes the Bible, puts it down softly and runs in without turning to look at Chellappan. She is going to the kitchen, of course. Is Thangaraj going to follow her there?

Chellappan smiles as he walks out.

Remembering My Mother

Professor J. Thampi Thankakumaran

My mother, Professor Hephzibah Jesudasan, was born on 9 April 1925 in Pulipunam—a small village in the Kanyakumari district, which is at the southern tip of the Indian peninsula. Both her father, Mr Thankakan, and her maternal grandfather Rev Devasahayam, were graduates. Her father believed in educating his daughters at a time when girls were considered incapable of becoming contributing citizens. While Amma took to teaching after her father and grandfather, her sister Beulah worked in the revenue department and retired as deputy tahsildar.

In her early childhood, Amma was never considered a good student. In fact, one of her Tamil teachers once remarked that she would never be able to learn Tamil, and if by any chance she did, she would do more harm than good to the language. My grandfather—her father—was always supportive of her. As a young girl, she went to Burma with her parents when her father took up a teaching job there. On returning to India, she joined the Duthie Girls School in Nagercoil. There, she met Ms Olive Morton, a missionary from England, who encouraged her, mentored her and helped her develop her writing skills. She went to the Scott Christian College to pursue her Intermediate degree, which was where she was recognized as a budding poet. Later, she joined University College in Thiruvananthapuram to get her bachelor's degree. She was the topper of her class. (Mr K.R. Narayanan, who later became the President of India was a year senior to her.)

She married Professor Jesudasan, a Tamil scholar, in 1947. My father encouraged her to write in Tamil, which led her to put together her childhood memories in the form of a novel. A neighbour of hers, who had also spent her childhood in Kanyakumari, was impressed by the style. This book, *Putham Veedu*, was not written in the language of the elite, but the language of the palmyra climbers—the very community she came from. She also wrote three other novels—*Ma Ni, Dr Chellappa* and *Anathai*.

Amma began her career as a teacher of English at the Government Women's College and was considered an excellent motivator. Teaching was her passion. She taught Shakespeare and very often dramatized it. Every year, she contributed a poem to the college magazine. Her students included the Malayalam writer Sugada Kumari, the Princess HRH Gowri Lakshmi Bayi and several other people of renown. She also served as the head of the English Department in Maharajas College, Ernakulam, Government College, Pattambi, All Saints College, Thiruvananthapuram and, eventually, retired from University College, Thiruvananthapuram.

She was a stern disciplinarian. As chairman of the Examination Board of the University of Kerala, she was the custodian of the English exam papers. The room where the papers were kept was always under lock and key and out of bounds for us, her children.

She loved music and introduced Western music to us. My father was informally trained in Carnatic music. My brother, sister and I would wake up every morning to the sound of the veena. At dinner time, talk would invariably centre around literature with Appa and Amma making points to support their arguments. It was these arguments which later took the shape of two books on the history of Tamil literature.

The time for us children to chatter among ourselves was after Appa and Amma left the table. After retirement, our parents moved to Pulipunam. They were fond of walking. The two would always be seen together, going on walks, wielding umbrellas as their walking sticks.

Once, during my college days, Amma decided to buy me new shoes for my birthday. It so happened that I hadn't done very well in my physics paper. Feeling guilty, I told her I would get the shoes after I improved my scores. But she was very understanding and said that it was fine and asked me to order my new pair the very next day. Amma lived a very simple life. Whenever I reminisce about her, I think of her in her cotton sarees and rubber chappals.

The health of her three children always troubled her. I was written off by the doctors as weak. Amma hired someone to look after me, a person I called *ammumma*. She did a good job, and so Amma entrusted her with the responsibilities of the entire household. After I grew up, she wanted to leave but Amma told her that she was part of our family and asked her to stay on. Ammumma did not have a family of her own. Towards the end of her days, she was bedridden and Amma personally looked after her. When she died, she was buried as a family member.

Amma was often concerned about the welfare of the poor. She celebrated the birthdays of her children by preparing elaborate meals for the homeless and the derelict. Perhaps she did this to educate us, her children, and to inculcate a social conscience in us. After her retirement, she started a school for the underprivileged children of her locality. Not content with doing just that, she made sure that her grandchildren also studied there. The students were very fortunate to have experts teach them for little or no fees. It is a matter of great pride that the alumni of this school have continued to fare well.

Amma did not believe in the caste system. I wanted to marry someone from outside our community and Amma had no objections. She did not accept dowry for either of her two sons. And Amma and Appa never treated my wife like an outsider.

Putham House

Amma spent her last days with me in our house. She lived for ten years after Appa passed away. In her last year, she lost her memory after suffering a stroke. Amma died peacefully at home on 10 February 2012.

Glossary

Achu murukku	A deep fried snack
Adade/Appappa	Exclamation of surprise
Adichukootu	The tiled front portion of a traditional south Indian house, flanking the entrance and open on two sides
Akka	Elder sister; also older women
Akkani	Fresh, unfermented palmyra sap
Amma/Amme/ Ammai	Mother
Annan	Elder brother
Anni	Elder brother's wife
Appa/Appan	Father
Aranai	Skink
Ayya	Sir
Ayyo / Ayyaiyo	An exclamation of fear or shock
Chithappa	Father's younger brother
Chithi	Wife of father's younger brother or mother's younger sister.

Dei	A form of address for a boy
Ettikai	Fruit of the strychnine tree
Kali	A Hindu goddess
Kanji	Gruel
Kannammai	Grandmother
Kannapachi	Grandfather
Karthigai	A month in the Tamil calendar from the second-half of November to the first-half of December
Keerai	Spinach
Kutty	Little girl
Kuzhambu	Curry
Le	A form of address reserved for young boys and those inferior in status
Maargazhi	A month in the Tamil calendar from the second-half of December to the first-half of January
Mama	Maternal uncle or father-in-law or respected elder
Mapillai	Son-in-law
Mullai	A variety of jasmine flower
Nellikai/Nelli	Gooseberry
Nethili	Anchovy
Nungu	Edible kernel of tender palmyra fruit
Oi	An informal, familiar form of address used only for men
Onam	Harvest festival
Panaiyeri	Palmyra climber
Panampazham	Palmyra fruit

Glossary

Panamkizhangu	Palmyra tuber
Pathani	Fresh palmyra sap
Periamma/	Mother's elder sister or father's elder
Periammai	brother's wife
Periyappa	Father's elder brother
Periyavar	Elder
Pilley	A form of address for a child or a youngster or one inferior in social position
Rasathi	Princess
Thambi	Form of address for younger brother or a man younger in age
Thatha	Grandfather or old man
Theivame	Dear God!
Thinnai	Raised platform at the entrance of a house on which you can sit or lie down
Thondi	Basket woven out of palm leaves
Thotta chunungi	Touch-me-not plant
Vaidyar	Doctor
Vei	Informal form of address used only for men
Visiris	Fans made of palm leaves